Something Earned

A Friends To Lovers Work Place Romantic Comedy

Something Series
Book 2

Chiquita Dennie

304 Publishing Company

Latest Releases

Series

Struck in Love

The Early Years-A Prequel Short Story

Ruthless:Antonio and Sabrina Book 1

Savage: Antonio and Sabrina Book 2

Beast: Antonio and Sabrina Book 3

Captivated By His Love:Janice and Carlo

Brutal: Antonio and Sabrina Booke 4

Redemption: Antonio and Sabrina Book 5

Heart of Stone

Broken, Book 1 (Emery & Jackson)

A Valentine's Day Short Book 1.5 Emery & Jackson

Rebirth, Book 2 (Jordan and Damon)

Reveal, Book 3 (Angela and Brent)

Bottoms Up Book 3.5 Jessica and Joseph Short

Renew, Book 4 (Jessica and Joseph)

Cocky Billionaire Boys

Cocky Catcher (Cocky Billionaire Boys Book 1)

Bossy Billionaire (Cocky Billionaire Boys Book 2)

The Fuertes Cartel
Stolen (The Fuertes Cartel Book 1)
Saved (The Fuertes Cartel Book 2)
Betrayed (The Fuertes Cartel Book 3)
Carrington Cartel
Torn: The Carrington Cartel Book 1
Claim: The Carrington Cartel Book 2
Something
Something Gained: A Romantic Comedy Book 1
Something Earned: A Romantic Comedy Book 2

Pierce Motors
Refuel: (Pierce Motors Book l)
Pressure: Pierce Motors Book 2)
Summer Break
Summer Nights: (Summer Break Book 1)
TN Seal Security
Aydin: Book 1
Nasir: Book 2
Nicco: Book 3

Standalones
Until Serena(HEA World Novel)
Temptation
She's All I Need
I Deserve His Love
Mutual Agreement
Scoring with Sadie
Exposed (A Bodyguard Novel)
Love Shorts:A Collection of Short Stories
Red Light District(A Fantasy Romance Short)

Author Inspiration

"Never allow anyone to steal your joy. It doesn't matter how many times someone says you can't do something. Invest in yourself—even if it's just writing down what your goals and plans are. Starting small can lead to bigger things."

—Chiquita Dennie

Disclaimer

This work of fiction contains strong language and explicit sexual content and is only intended for mature readers. This story may contain unconventional situations, language, and sexual encounters that may offend some readers. This book is for mature readers (18+).

Introduction

Grab some wine and get ready for more spicy, sinful, sexy suspense.

Are you signed up for my newsletter?

Join today and find out all the latest in new releases, contests, giveaways, sneak peeks and more.

www.chiquitadennie.com

Synopsis

Kianna has worked hard and knows she deserves a promotion at the radio station, despite what all the naysayers in her life say.

Caleb has gone above and beyond to prove he can handle taking on more responsibilities at work. What he's not sure he's ready to handle is competing with Kianna for a job.

A promotion is up for grabs, but only one can have it. With ex-lovers, a relationship that's blurring the lines between coworkers, good friends, and lovers, Kianna and Caleb have a lot on their minds.

Can they ignore the outside distractions and focus on what matters, or will they jeopardize what could be the best thing that ever happened to them?

A Steamy Friends to Lovers, WorkPlace Romantic Comedy.

Chapter 1

Kianna

"Where did I put my notebook?" Often my family and friends thought I was crazy because I had to talk out loud in order to clarify my thoughts. The mess in my trunk made me tap my finger on my cheek, scan my car's trunk, and walk toward the front groaning.

"Yo! Kianna, what are you doing?" My heart skipped a beat when I heard his boisterous voice.

I rolled my eyes, knowing he would find me and ask a dumb question. The confused look on his face made me smile wide from the backseat as I leaned forward. My best friend, Caleb, had to always be in my business, no matter what was going on in his day.

Motioning at the car, I asked, "What does it look like Caleb?" I scanned his fresh attire for work today.

Raking a hand to scratch the little ingrown hair on his chin, he shrugged. "Hell if I know when it comes to you." He smirked and wagged a finger at me.

I pushed off the door. "For your information, I lost my notebook."

"The famous notebook," he said, putting his hands up in air quotes and laughing.

I hit his chest lightly. "Shut up and help me look."

"Alright, little girl. I got five minutes to spare," Caleb grumbled, walking around to the truck.

"What happens in five minutes?" With the clutter I had accumulated over the past few weeks, I tossed the shoes to the front seat. As a result of working, making time for friends, and helping my mom move stuff around the house, I was exhausted.

"We got that meeting for the new promoter job at the station." A bra was raised by Caleb, and I quickly snatched it and put it away.

"Gimme that," I spat, watching him laugh at me. We both got hired at the same time at the radio station, and we never let it get in between our friendship. I stomped my feet like a little brat and poked my lip out in a pout. I hated when he laughed at me.

He shook his head. "Don't snap at me because you have a house in your car." I watched Caleb flip through my gold and black notebook. I grabbed it back before he could see anything I wrote. The notebook contained a lot of my plans, from my college days to my retirement.

"Thank you, Caleb." I stuck my tongue out at him.

He pinched my cheek with a smile. "Yeah, whatever, brat."

"Are you ready for work? I mean, we're both competing for the same position." I reminded him of the competition he would face.

Shutting and locking the door, I lifted my book bag onto my shoulder.

"Born ready, brat." Caleb ruffled my hair.

I pushed his hands off my freshly done braids. "I got your brat."

Once we checked in for the day, I lifted the vanilla latte to my lips and rested back in my seat as the director of our radio station went on about the latest numbers from our audience live event. For the past two years, I've worked at this radio station in the promo department, and I wanted the new position as program director. I felt a nudge to my left elbow and glanced over to Caleb, pretending to be asleep. As a voice cleared, I giggled at his antics and covered my mouth.

Cheston, our boss, inquired, "Is something funny, Kianna?"

Sitting straight up in my seat, I reached under the table and pinched Caleb on the thigh for getting me in trouble.

"No, sir." I cleared my throat, put my coffee on the table, and pretended to write notes. These meetings ran on for hours, and everyone complained, but Cheston refused to keep them short. He had no idea what I brought to him, I never got a thumbs up or a nice job, Kianna. It felt like he hated how much everybody loved me at the station. Cheston was only in his mid-thirties and for the most part he'd brought in a few radio announcers to help expand our numbers. At the same time it was the same boring music and nothing new or exciting with the younger crowd like me.

"If something is funny, please tell everyone." His face turned red in aggravation, and he gestured around the room. A few people snickered under their breaths.

"Well, sir... Ouch!" I jumped up, knocking the coffee on my lap, and I glared at Caleb for sticking me with his pen.

"If you plan on going out for the Director role, I suggest you do better than what we see today," Cheston chastised, flipping the whiteboard. I wiped off my pants, dropped my cup in the trash, and slouched back into the seat.

"Asshole," I said, pretending to cough and whispering under my breath.

A few people around me laughed and Cheston's head whipped around. Everyone shut up again. The position not only came with a raise, but my dream had always been to work in radio with my own show that broke out new artists. I went to college for journalism and while I was there, music theater intrigued me. At the same time, I watched my cousin go for her dreams as a chemist. The meeting finished and everybody disbursed out of the room. Caleb went into the employee lounge, while I headed to my cubicle area. Taking a seat, I logged into the computer and checked my emails and noticed management was setting up interview times. I gathered my ringing phone with my cousin's name scrolled across. She was happily in love in California living her best life.

I leaned back in my chair and took the call. "Hey, favorite cousin."

"I miss you, Kianna," Ava sighed, laughing in the background.

"Miss you more. How is California?"

"Fun, chaotic with work," Ava moaned.

"I bet, overseeing so many businesses and having a crazy family and man."

I turned at the tap on my shoulder. Caleb stood next to me with a folder in his hand. "Hold on, Ava. Caleb is bugging me." I stuck my tongue out at him.

"Tell Caleb I said hi!" Ava mentioned.

"What's up?"

His brows drew together. "What are we doing for lunch?"

"Can we go to the sandwich shop around the corner?"

"Alright, hurry up and be ready on time, or I'm leaving your ass," Caleb joked and squeezed my cheek, a habit he'd had for the past few years that pissed me off. I smacked his hand down and went back to my call with Ava.

"When are you going to stop fighting how you feel about him?"

I felt a lump rise in my throat. "Feel about who?"

"Girl, you're a mess."

Exhaling, I logged in my receipts from our last festival event. "Have no idea what you are talking about."

"You like Caleb."

My heart skipped a beat. "No, I don't."

"You two would be cute together," Ava teased.

Ava's always tried to put me and Caleb together as a couple. Most of our family thought we'd be married with kids by now. At my age of twenty five, I was not interested in the life of a husband, car, and two kids. Staying on top of getting my promotion, becoming the top in my field, and maybe one day becoming a talk show host were the only goals I had set for myself. Love could wait.

I groaned and logged out of the email chain. "Did I tell you Matt tried to call me about going to dinner?" I informed her while I reached for my purse, keys, and backpack from under my chair. I waved at another colleague.

"Ex-boyfriend Matt?" Ava asked.

I went down the hall to meet Caleb at the elevator. I saw him talking with Ralesha, another girl that worked here. So many times she'd tried to get Caleb's attention and thought we were a couple. Since then, a hatred for me has seeped into her mind.

My skin prickled with alarm. "Let me call you back, Ava."

"Fine, call me later. I might be coming into town," Ava said.

"Keep me updated and we can have a girls' night. Shiva won't mess with you."

"Broomhilda aka Shiva is possessed, always running around like she is Spiderman, climbing the walls."

I snickered at her hate for my baby. "Leave my cat alone. She's sweet."

"She ain't sweet. She got 666 scrolled across her head," Ava answered, sounding annoyed.

The elevator door swung open. I pushed my phone back into my pocket and stepped onto the platform.

"Hello, Kianna," Ralesha sneered.

I grinned and put on my best fake smile. "Oh, hey, Ralesha." Her lip peeled back. She sucked into her teeth with a frown at my presence.

"Anyway, Caleb. How about we do lunch together?" Ralesha flirted, pressing her palms to his chest. Both of us were around the same height of five-six, to Caleb's five-eleven. Caleb released a breath and pushed his hands in his pockets. He grinned wide for her and it pissed me off. The dimples that I liked to poke when I'm bored sprang wide, and I felt a little jealous for the first time that he was paying her attention. Finally we got off on the main floor. I stretched my hand out and popped him in the back of the head, then ran to his car and jumped in the driver's seat.

"What the fuck, Kianna?" Caleb grumbled, swiping the back of his neck.

"You got five minutes before I leave you!" I spat.

"Stop playing and get in the passenger seat."

"Caleb! What about me?" Ralesha snapped, crossing her arms.

Climbing in the car, I adjusted the passenger seat as Caleb got situated. He closed the door and ignored Ralesha.

I giggled and checked the messages on my phone. "Better answer your girlfriend."

"Shut up, big head. That's not my girlfriend." He started the car.

Scoffing, I double checked my hair and put the camera on so I could take a selfie. "Are you sure she knows that? I can't tell by the way she hangs on your every word."

He snatched my phone away. When he stopped at a red light, he scrolled through my photo album.

"Positive." Seeing the light change, he drove through the light, turned right, and pulled up to the front entrance of the restaurant. Instead of giving me my phone, he slid it into his pocket.

"Give me my phone back!" I wiggled my left hand at him.

"Nope, it's my time now." Caleb extended his arm around my neck. He leaned his head down and placed a kiss on my forehead.

I wiped his kiss away, even though I loved forehead kisses. I didn't want to show any emotion. "Ugh, you get on my nerves." I was at the location and parked a few minutes later.

"Love you too." Cackling, he opened the door for me to walk in first.

The hostess greeted us, since we come here often, and took us to a table in the back. Sliding in the booth, Caleb climbed in next to me, shoving me over as the hostess laid the menus down on the table.

"Can I get a little breathing room?" I chided.

Caleb lifted his hand to remove his shades. "Girl, hush. You know you love me next to you."

"If you weren't my best friend, I would cut you." Caleb laughed and pinched my cheek. "Ouch, asshole." I rubbed the sting from my cheek.

He ignored my comment. "What's Ava talking about today?"

"None of your business."

He raised a hand to stroke his jaw. "One day that mouth of yours is going to get you in trouble."

"Not today though," I said with a wink of my left eye just as the waitress came to our table to greet us.

Caleb's light brown skin burned red with annoyance, and I didn't know why until she opened her mouth.

"Caleb, really?" The waitress grimaced.

Groaning, Caleb leaned back in the booth, glaring at her with disdain.

I pointed between the both of them. "Do you two know each other?"

She rested a hand on her hip. "He knows me really well, especially when he fucks me and doesn't call me back," she argued.

"Sharice, keep moving. You knew what it was that night," Caleb reminded her.

"Caleb, you promised you would call!" Sharice snapped.

I lifted a finger in the air and looked around the cafe for help. "Umm can I get another waitress?"

She stared from me to Caleb with a glare and walked off in a huff, smacking her lips. Caleb looked down at the menu acting like nothing was happening.

"Hello, are you not going to talk about Sharice?"

He tugged on his ear, which was something he did when he was lying about something or trying to avoid a conversation. Caleb blew out a breath. "I had a one night stand with the girl. No big deal." He shrugged and reached for his water. Sharice walked back over with another girl beside her and placed our drinks on the table.

"Here's your Coke and Sprite." Sharice grunted, popping straws on the table.

"Actually, can we get an unopened bottle of Sprite?" I asked while shoving the glass back to her.

She hiked her brow with a snarl. "What are you saying? I spit in your drink or something?" Sharice demanded with a glower.

Confrontation was my specialty, and she met the wrong one today. "Yes."

"Come on, Sharice. Let it go," Caleb groaned as he dragged a hand down his face.

My gaze slid from him to her, and the poor waitress next to her looked shocked at our situation.

Smirking evilly, Sharice picked up both glasses, held them over Caleb's head, and poured them out. I jumped in our seat with an angry shout. I tried to get out of the booth to throw the water, but Caleb wrapped his arms around my waist.

The bitch had the nerve to cackle as she walked off. Caleb apologized to the other waitress and hauled me along to leave the restaurant. A muscle ticked in his jaw.

He got into the car and slammed the door shut. I wiped my clothes down with napkins that were in the console.

"You owe me lunch and dinner."

"I already know you're going to make me pay for that."

I counted down my wants on my hands. "Oh you have no idea. I want foot rubs, massages, and you're going to feed me grapes."

Laughing at me, Caleb drove us back to the station, driving his Jeep Wrangler and parking in the employee section. Hopping out, he came around to open the door for me and slapped a high five.

Stepping back in the building and going through security, my stomach growled letting me know I needed to eat.

"Kianna, you look lovely today." Bernard, a security guard on duty, shamefully licked his lips. Pretty much since I started at the station, he's flirted with me, and a few times I did talk with him during lunch breaks in the employee lounge. He felt more like a friend rather than a guy I could see myself dating.

"Keep your eyes up here, my guy." Caleb gripped me by the shoulders as he walked us to the elevator.

"He was being nice."

"Yeah, right."

"Don't get jealous." I pushed the button for our floor.

Caleb remarked, "Bernard's not your type."

I swiveled around to face him. "And what's my type?"

Before he could answer my question the doors opened. We stepped onto a crowded elevator. We moved to the corner, but more people stepped on, shoving Caleb forward and almost knocking me down. Caleb put both his hands on my hips, his chest to my back. I felt his dick on my butt. I had never checked out his package before. I had always looked at him as a friend. I was shaking my thoughts away when he slowly tugged me closer with his palm on my stomach. I attempted to move out of his grip, sure he had made a mistake, but in the next moment, he pushed me flush to his chest. The weird arousal churned between us and sent a shock up my spine.

Chapter 2

Caleb

Once the weekend rolled around, a few of my guy friends and I gathered at my apartment for a night of poker and drinks. I hadn't heard from Kianna for a few days, which was unusual for us since we usually talked every day on the phone, even while at work. After shuffling the cards, Lamar came out with the large pizzas and hot wings we ordered. Working at the station hadn't afforded me the rich lifestyle, but I managed to get a nice two bedroom apartment thanks to money from my family. Growing up in a middle class Boston family, my parents worked hard to put me and my sister through school.

"Alright, what are we betting?" Lamar chomped down on hot wings, chugging beer.

"Man, if you don't take your ass in the kitchen and eat." They all knew I hated to have something spill on my furniture and floors. My place was decorated by Kianna with grays and cream colors with a masculine feel, a few flowers and artwork here and there.

Lamar mumbled under his breath, then got up to sit at

the island away from the card table. Music blasted and Oscar lit the cigar, taking a few puffs, ashing it out when I glared at him, raising his hands up in surrender.

Oscar apologized and moved the ashtray closer. "Sorry, man. I forgot"

"Told you to take that shit outside on the balcony."

"What's gotten into you, bro?" Lamar called me out.

I frowned in deep thought. "Nothing."

"Nawl, something's up. Your parents?" Lamar investigated.

"No."

Oscar hopped on the questioning train. "Your sister asking for money?"

"No." It was irritating to be questioned.

"Kianna." Lamar chuckled and wiped his hands on the napkins.

As usual I could not hide when I was lying. I avoided eye contact with Lamar and rubbed the back of my head.

Lamar lifted his fist to his mouth with a grin. "Oh, shit! It's Kianna? What did you do?"

"Did you come here to play poker or gossip?" I argued, shuffling my hand.

"Kianna pissed him off and he's taking it out on us." Lamar clowned, almost choking on his food.

"Fuck you."

"Sorry but I will let Kianna do that for you." Lamar winked.

Flipping him off, all the guys burst into laughter. "For real, bro, tell us what happened." Oscar got up and grabbed some food.

I cleared my throat and thought back to the other day in the office of being close to her in the elevator. For the longest time I've had a crush on Kianna, and I hid it well, but smelling her sweet perfume and feeling her soft skin under my touch sparked those feelings again. I know some people believe men and women couldn't be friends and normally I would agree, but ever since college, I watched Kianna come out of her shell while I watched every guy lust over her. All along I knew how sweet, funny, and caring she was. It only made me want her more. When she was happy, I loved being around her energy. Even when she's sad, I found a way to make her smile.

At the loud banging on my door, we all stopped what we were doing. I stood to answer the door. I snatched it open to see Kianna standing in front of me wearing the shortest dress I'd ever seen with her breasts practically spilling out. My eyes narrowed into slits.

"Why are you banging on my door, and where the hell are your clothes?"

Kianna pushed me to the side and marched into my place with her friends behind her all dressed like they were going out to the club.

"You promised to let me use your car since mine is in the shop." She held out her palm for the keys, but I slapped her hand down.

A look of scorn flashed across my face. "Not dressed like that."

"Caleb, you promised," she whined, stomping her foot.

I listened to her girls giggling and my boys laughing as I pushed Kianna down the hall and to my bedroom so we could talk alone. "Stop pushing me." Kianna shoved me away, and I shut and locked my bedroom door. I leaned against it with my arms folded.

My face hardened and my dick twitched. I put both

hands in front of me to not be obvious. I was glad I was wearing shorts over my boxers and then my sweats. "Go change."

Looking down at her dress, Kianna smirked. "Why? Jealous?"

"You know what you are doing, Kianna."

"What am I doing?" She raised her hand to her chest, clutching her invisible pearls despite her mocking tone.

"Keep playing with me."

She cupped her ear and bent forward. "I'm sorry. Is my name Sharice?"

Licking my lips, I pushed off the door and crowded her space. I planted my hands on both sides of her body, locking her in place. Her breaths increased and got heavier.

"Do you want to be Sharice?"

She waved me off. "I don't know what you are talking about."

"I see it now. You're jealous."

Her face crinkled in confusion. "Huh?"

"If you want to test out the package, Bug, just tell me." My nickname for Kianna was bug, because she always bugged me about something and like a fool I did everything she asked, from taking her car to get fixed, picking her up from the hair salon, to making sure no guys ever attempted to hurt her. then I'd step in if any fool tried. Hell, I have even given her money for shopping. We were truly best friends. She helped me out with studying for school. She's cooked dinner a few nights out of the week.

"I hate that nickname."

"Too bad."

"For your information, I would never want to try out

that little wiener. I like them big, long, and thick." She tried to stand up, but I gently pushed her flat on her back on my bed.

"Yo! Kianna make some noise if you need rescuing. I got the police on speed dial," Lamar yelled, causing everybody to laugh.

"Shut up, Lamar!" I scoffed.

Kianna smirked to herself and nudged me away. She rose from the bed and tugged her sexy dress down. I felt my dick throb in my sweats. I adjusted myself and stood, walked to the dresser, and passed her my car keys.

"Here, and you better call me once you get there and when you're on your way back."

"I can manage, Dad."

"Yeah, whatever. Still need to change clothes."

"All the girls are wearing this bodycon dress." Kianna yanked the door open, Lamar and Oscar almost fell inside.

"My bad, bro. Oscar said he heard a scream and we wanted to make sure Kianna wasn't beating you," Lamar joked.

"Fuck you, Lamar," Kianna jested as she held her hand up to me. I knew she would ask for more than the keys to my car. Of course, she would.

"What?" I smacked her palm in a high five.

"I need money for drinks. Kizzie got the section for us," Kianna informed me.

I stuffed my hand in my pocket, took out three hundred dollars, and put it in her hand. "Damn! I wish I had a best friend like that," Lamar exclaimed.

"Get the fuck on, Lamar." We followed Kianna out front to the living room and she waved for her friends to follow.

"Thanks, best friend!" Kianna yelled, leaving my apartment. Taking a seat back at the card table, all eyes were on me. "What?" I reshuffled the deck of cards.

"Are we not going to talk about how you just gave your best friend the keys to your car and money to go out and potentially meet guys?" Lamar quizzed.

"Give me five minutes." I dropped the cards on the table and rushed to the bedroom to change. I heard them howl in laughter. Hearing the entire situation really had me fucked in the head but I let myself ignore how I really felt about Kianna.

* * *

Raven, Kianna's other best friend, stood with a drink in the air, rolling her hips to the music, scoping out the scene around the club. I motioned for Lamar and Oscar to follow me up the stairs to where Kianna said they had a section. *Kream* was sweltering hot from the amount of bodies filling the place and rubbing up against each other with music blasting in the air. I scanned the area looking for her. My nostrils flared at the scene before me. Kianna was sitting in some guy's lap, giggling at his fake ass conversation. I was never the jealous type but knowing she was too good for him, I stalked over, reached for her hand, and pulled her out of his grasp.

"Aye, the fuck, man!" he shouted.

"Caleb! What is your problem?" Kianna screamed. I shoved her behind me when the dude stood up to press me.

"She's taken." I knew my friends and hers looked at me like I was crazy, because we were only friends. I grew more aggravated when I watched his hands drag across her silky brown skin, and she laughed at his jokes like she had done at mine.

"Caleb, if you don't—" Kianna started to speak, and I lifted her over my shoulder and walked out of their section to our own VIP seats across the way. I weaved through the people, and Kianna kept hitting me on the back. I smacked her on the ass lightly.

"Ouch! Caleb..." She wiggled to be let down. I forced a bottle of water in her hands.

"Drink," I ordered.

"A party pooper."

"King of the party, baby." Lamar and Oscar shook their heads at me.

"Caleb, you are killing our vibe." Raven and Kizzie argued. They took a seat next to her, not waiting long to grab up the bottle of Ciroc and making a drink.

"As usual, your captain saves a hoe," Sharice baited the girls. I was caught off guard when Kianna jumped up, threw the water, then the ice from the bucket, at Sharice, soaking her clothes.

"Oooohhh...Sharice, I know you ain't letting her get away with that." A friend of Sharice's pumped her up.

"Bitch!" Sharice lunged at Kianna. I jumped out of my seat but not quick enough to separate the girls as they rolled around on the floor. Kianna had her flat on the ground, punching her in the face.

"Kianna, that's enough. Come on, Bug."

"You just mad he don't want your funky ass!" Kianna shouted, smacking Sharice in the head.

"Lamar, help me separate them and stop filming, bro."

"Shit, I can sell this on OnlyFans or something. Show a little titty, Kianna!" Lamar joked.

I growled and took the phone out of his hand. He chuckled and helped me remove Kianna from Sharice.

"Let me go!" Kianna screamed. I carried her out of the club to get some space between them and to let her cool down. Holding her up against my car, I smoothed her hair down on her head, while she continued to fuss.

The shrieking familiar voice screamed, "Caleb how can you leave and not pay for my hair and clothes to get fixed." Sharice had followed us outside.

Giggling with so much malice, Kianna started to argue with Sharice, but I crushed my lips to hers. It shocked me. Not only because of how sweet and soft her lips felt, but I heard her moans and felt her arms link around my neck. It shocked everyone who was watching as well.

"Damn! I guess that is his girl," Lamar blurted out.

"Fuck you, Caleb!" Sharice shouted, marching away and complaining with her friends.

Feeling her arms lower, Kianna shoved me back. She rubbed her lips and stared at me in surprise.

"You good, Kianna?" Kizzie called out.

"Uh, yeah. I'm ready to go home."

There was so much disappointment in her eyes, and I fucking hated it. I went to grab her wrist, but she pulled away and stumbled back. "Kianna, let me drive you home."

"No, I need a minute. Lamar, can you drop us off, please?" Kianna asked my boy, and I sobered up quickly.

Watching her dip out on me with Lamar, Oscar motioned me to his car and I dragged my palm down my face. I was so fucking aggravated at Sharice's dumb ass.

"I can tell you're not ready to talk about it, but is that the first time y'all kissed?" Oscar inquired.

"Yeah, man." I blew out a breath and stared out of the window.

Smacking his teeth, Oscar followed Lamar out of the parking lot and turned up the music to let me think over my thoughts.

* * *

Early morning light filled my bedroom. I finally opened my eyes at the loud laughter in my apartment. I already knew who the culprit would be, sneaking in without a warning and not caring if I had guests or not. I pulled on my sweats and strolled into the bathroom to brush my teeth. I rubbed my eyes and stood in the hallway, watching my mom laughing with my auntie. I leaned over and gave her a kiss on the cheek and hug. I did same for my Auntie Daria who was checking her makeup. I took the stool next to my auntie, grabbed the bag of food on the counter, and grabbed a homemade bacon and egg sandwich.

Stretching my arms, I rubbed my grumbling stomach. "That key is for emergencies only."

My mother stood at the edge of the kitchen island. "Boy looks just like his father. So damn handsome but aggravates the shit out of me," my mother teased me and walked to the fridge for a gallon of milk.

I covered my mouth and laughed as she rolled her eyes. Angel had my dad's head gone from the first day they met in high school.

"Good one, Angel."

She glared at me when I called her by her name, something she hated when I tried to get on her nerves.

"Keep playing with me, Caleb, and your big headed ass will be shipped off to boarding school."

I took a glass out of the cabinet and opened the milk, filled the glass, and gulped it down. "I think I aged out of boarding school, ma'am."

"Not where I'm sending you." She winked at me.

"Auntie, get your sister." I pointed at my mom and sat back down on the stool.

"Nephew, you know I love you, but I let my little sister handle her own affairs," Auntie Daria emphasized, and we both knew that was a lie.

"Daria, stop lying. Your ass is in everybody's business. Gossip in the clinic was started by you." Mom waved her off and burst into loud laughter. My auntie rolled her eyes knowing she was right. She worked at the same hospital as my dad, the place my mom worked for a few years until she had me and became a stay at home mom. Auntie had everybody's secrets spread around the entire hospital.

"She's right."

Mom and I high fived, laughing at my Auntie ignoring us while she played on her phone. I finished off the breakfast sandwich, wiped my hands, and cleaned up my trash. I knew what was coming, so I leaned on the counter waiting for the shoe to drop.

"How are you doing, baby boy?" Mom asked.

Angel started off her investigations of what was going on in my life with the same style of seeing how I was feeling and then counteracting with how I need to be giving her grandbabies before she gets too old.

"Mom, let's cut to the chase. Why are you here at eight in the morning?"

She threw a hand on her hip and narrowed her eyes. "Can I not visit my son to check on his well-being?"

"No," Auntie and I answered at the same time.

"Daria, I told you to stay in the car anyway," Mom chastised.

"Girl, leave me out of this mess," Auntie replied.

Both my mom and auntie were in their fifties, with dark brown skin, an athletic build, and youthful looking. Sometimes people thought I was her boyfriend and she was a cougar because she looked to be in her late thirties.

"Ignore Daria. Your dad is having a big fundraiser at the hospital, and he wants you to come."

Groaning, I dropped my head on the counter, pretending to not hear her request. "Ma, you know I hate those dinners."

"Which is why I think it will be nice to bring a date. I know a few girls or invite Kianna as your plus one."

Angel made Kianna feel right at home when they met, even to the point of calling her a daughter in law. I had to constantly tell her nothing was going on with us, but deep down she knew I had feelings for Kianna and was afraid to admit it out loud and lose our friendship.

"Not happening." I rose from the stool and headed to my bedroom, but she stopped me at the door.

Mom tilted her head to the side. "Why not?"

"I'm busy."

"Too busy for the woman who was in labor for over ten hours delivering a nine pound, big headed boy?" Mom reminded me, as usual, through emotional blackmail.

"Ma!"

"Fine! Destroy your poor father's heart." She pretended to clutch her invisible pearls around her neck.

Throwing my head back, I closed my eyes and groaned. Loudly. This woman. "Send me the date and time, Ma. I cannot promise anything."

"Thank you, sweetie!" Mom jumped up to kiss me on the cheek. I chuckled, then bent down a little to let her kiss me on the cheek.

"Yeah, yeah, yeah. Tell your husband you need to get back to work or find a better hobby."

"My hobby is riding his—"

I raised my palm to cut her off. "Get out!" I shouted as I slammed my door and listened to them cackle as they left my apartment.

Chapter 3

Kianna

Sunday rolled around and I was stuck at my parents' house listening to my mom complain about her neighbors not cutting their grass in a specific way. Geraldine Berry had it in her mind that everybody should live according to a certain lifestyle that only shows the perfect world God created. Unfortunately no one was perfect and no matter how many times she tried to dictate my life or anyone else's, it had to be said. Pushing my shades over my eyes, I sipped on the coffee, took in her words, and nodded, pretending like it made sense.

"Do you see what I'm saying, KiKi?"

"Uh huh." I yawned, pocketing my phone.

"Are you even listening?"

"Yep."

She stepped up on the stairs after getting the mail. "What did I say?"

"Something about the grass." I scratched my forehead and finished off my espresso.

"Kianna! I know you see me over here." Mr. Roger

shouted from across the street. He came out of his house and sat on the porch. He's an older man in his late seventies, with fake teeth and a cane. He tried to flirt with me every time I showed up. It was harmless and I loved to get under my mom's skin. The both of them hated each other, but I found it funny when they went back and forth.

I waved a hand in the air. "Hi, Mr. Roger!" I shouted back, ignoring my mom.

"Hey, baby. Are you coming to dinner tonight?" His nurse came out of the door, handing him a glass of water and some pills.

"Stop talking to his old ass." Mom propped a hand on the door handle.

I shook my head. "He's sweet and lonely. You know he only gets visits from the nurse."

"Why are you wearing glasses on a nice day?"

"Tired from work."

The nurse went back inside. "Tell that boyfriend of yours a real man is waiting." Mr. Roger coughed, holding his chest, and stood to do his signature one two step.

"Roger, leave my daughter alone!" Mom yelled. "Well if you stopped working at that radio business and got a job at the church, you'd be rested."

I chortled at the frown on her face. "Mr. Roger, I don't know if I can handle you." I faced her. "Ma, you don't even believe that lie."

She raised the stack of mail in her hand and smacked me on top of the head. "Ouch! Why'd you hit me? For telling the truth?"

"Stop hitting my future wife!" Mr. Roger stumbled back in his chair.

"Roger, if you want to see another day, you better stay out of my business," Mom challenged him.

Mr. Roger put up his fists, ready to box, mouth jerked into a grin.

Mom waved off his fighting stance. "Girl, shut up and come in the house. We need to prepare for dinner."

"Ma, Sunday dinner isn't for another seven hours." I got up and pulled on my shorts. She shook her head.

A loud whistle came from across the street. "Don't hurt nobody with those hips, Kianna." Mr. Roger kept flirting with me, ignoring my mom's glare.

"If you're early, you will never be late, and besides, Angel is coming tonight. You know I have to be on point." My mother had a competitiveness with Angel from what I gathered because Angel loved me and treated me like a daughter. We had gotten really close over the years. I could say sometimes I had gone to her first with my thoughts and feelings before I would talk with my mom because she never made me feel judged. Even my dad, when he's not agreeing with Mom, would sometimes give me advice to not live in their shadows, but Mom had to control everything in her path. Caleb's parents and mine met on campus when we became friends and often hung out when we were not around, especially when my dad found out he could go golfing for free based on the Glover last name.

I was throwing my coffee cup in the trash when I felt my cell phone vibrate in my pocket. I took it out and lifted the phone and saw Caleb's name on the screen. I sighed when his message popped up.

Caleb: We need to talk.

I knew he wanted to bring up the kiss from last night. At first my alcohol intake had me confused on what we'd done, but a small part of me loved the feel of his plump lips on top of mine and his strong hands holding me tight.

If his little bitch, Sharice, hadn't interrupted my evening, I would have been going home with a new little friend. But Caleb's protective nature had always come out when someone he cared about was being threatened.

Me: About?

Caleb: Stop playing bug.

Me: I hate that nickname.

Caleb: Then let's talk about it 🙂

Me: Not slick jerk.

"Kianna, grab the potatoes and start cutting." Mom motioned toward the fridge, then sat down at the table.

Caleb: Seriously, my place movie night.

Me: We have dinner with you parents tonight.

Caleb: Even better, I can drive us back home.

Me: Pump your brakes, Sir. I have plans.

Caleb: With who?

Me: None of your business. I'm being summoned.

Caleb: Tell Momma Geraldine I read the scripture today.

I chuckled at his message. "Liar," I mumbled under my breath as I typed it as a reply.

"What are you laughing at, child?"

I glanced at her. "Caleb said he read the Bible today."

She clasped her hands together in prayer pose and closed her eyes. "Thank you, Jesus."

Me: You got her over here praying over your lies.

Caleb: Doing more for the church than you.

I giggled at the screenshot he sent of him sitting on the balcony of his apartment with the Bible open and the football game on his iPad.

I closed my texts and plopped down next to Mom at the table. "Have you heard from Ava?" I wondered.

"Jamie said Ava and Blaze are doing good, still working in that science stuff."

"Science stuff," I snickered, rolling up the sleeves of my hoodie.

"Anyway, how hungover are you this time?"

I wasn't expecting that and the question caught me off guard. I paused, trying to think of a new lie. "Hungover?" I pursed my lips at her and stood up from the table to pick up the potatoes to wash in the sink.

"Kianna, you can never get one over on me, child. I was your age once."

"Geraldine, where's my breakfast?" Daddy strolled in the kitchen wearing a house robe, boxers, and white-t shirt that stretched over his protruding belly.

"Titus, I told you to shower and get out there to cut the lawn."

Dad kissed me on the back of my head and I wrapped an arm around his waist. "Hi, Daddy."

Dad slapped my mom on the butt. "Hey, bug."

"Really, Daddy?"

"What?"

"Caleb made you call me bug?" I cocked my hip out and glared at him.

"Pumpkin, you bug that man and I have no doubt he enjoys your annoyance," he commented. My mouth opened and closed rapidly. Did he really say that?

"Titus, worry about the garden before our guests arrive and leave your child alone," my mom demanded.

"Yes, dear." Dad picked up his plate of breakfast and strolled out the kitchen, not caring at all that my mother was snarling at him.

"I will kill Caleb," I grunted. I turned off the faucet and slid back down in the chair. Most of our friends and a few family members knew I was spoiled, but I still worked my ass off to have nice things. Like right now my apartment was purchased by my parents, but I worked to keep up the maintenance. I tossed my braids behind my back, removed my cap, and listened to Mom harmonize her favorite singer, Shirley Caesar.

I swallowed down my nervousness to open the conversation I'd been avoiding. "I'm up for a promotion."

Her left brow arched up. "At the radio station?"

I fidgeted in my seat under her hard gaze. "Yes, ma'am."

Sighing, she scooted the green beans to the side and gave me her full attention. "What's the promotion?"

My insides trembled with the hope she might really be interested in my dreams, so I started to ramble. "Well, it would be for Program Director. Basically I would be setting up the layout of what the listeners would hear on the radio."

"How much does it pay?"

"Mom, it's not all about money!"

A low clipped sound came from her lips. "Kianna, how many times are you going to put yourself in a dead-end job?"

"My dreams aren't a dead end!"

Mom slammed her fist down on the table. "You will not yell in my house."

I bit down on my lip and lowered my eyes. "Yes, ma'am."

"I understand you like to do the opposite of what I say, so all I can give you is the real truth of the world. Nothing is promised."

"Is there more you want to tell me, Geraldine?"

"Call me Geraldine again," she hissed, throwing a green bean at me.

Laughing at the frown on her face, I scooted over and kissed her on the cheek, then pulled her into a light hug. "Sorry for yelling."

"I'm sorry, too, baby. I love you and want you to be okay when your father and I aren't here."

As soon as she got into a conversation of me being good when they were no longer around, I knew it would drag on until it was dinner time.

* * *

Caleb bumped me with his shoulder right when he walked into my parents' house. I had finished prep for dinner early, so I showered in my old room and changed clothes. Even though I moved out for college over five years ago, I kept a few things there for when I spent the night after going to church on Sundays. Angel and Zamari Glover greeted my mom with flowers and handed Dad a bottle of wine as a thank you.

Reaching her arms out for a hug, I ran into Angel's embrace and giggled at her excitement. "Little girl, why have you not called me?" she demanded. I felt bad. With work and living life, I had forgotten my weekly catch up with Angel. Sometimes we went and got our hair and nails done together. A few times my mom would join us, but mostly it was a thing just the two of us would do for bonding.

"Mrs. Glover, I'm sorry. Work has kept me busy."

She frowned and tapped me on the butt. "Cut that Mrs. Glover mess and call me Angel," she demanded. She drew me in close and we walked to the couch. Caleb stood with his father and my dad talking about sports and the hype with the Super Bowl next year.

"Sorry, Angel."

Mom walked away carrying the wine and flowers to the kitchen. "Now, catch me up. My son said you've been avoiding him," Angel confessed.

"That's not true."

"Then tell me your side of things."

"Nothing to tell. Work. We're both up for a Promotions Director position at the radio station."

"Oooh, that's nice. Any dates lately?"

Ignoring my work comment, Angel thought she was slick bringing up my dating life with everybody standing around us. "No, I have a few people I might be interested in talking with, but right now I am focused on my career."

"Glad to hear you're staying on top of your career. The men will come when it's time. Besides, you can get a little friends with benefits on the side."

"Angel Glover!" Caleb yelled, grimacing at his mom.

"Caleb," Angel responded. Her mouth moved into a teasing quirk at the corner of her mouth.

"Pops, get your woman." Caleb reached down, lifted me up so he could sit, and then put me on his lap. I tried to scoot over to give him space, but he grasped my waist tight. Angel and I made eye contact, and she grinned at me with a tight smile.

"Angel, leave those kids alone." Mr. Glover, for an older man, was sexy and I could see why Angel kept her eyes on every woman that came around her husband.

Zamari Glover was not only tall, but leanly built, and had a deep sexy voice. He let Angel be Angel, until she got too wild, and he would put her in her place if she crossed the line. Zamari was gorgeous with Light brown skin, low curly hair, gray strands in his beard, and deep hazelnut eyes, broad shoulders, and long legs. He could put any woman in a trance. It did not hurt that he was an orthopedic surgeon.

"Caleb is the one causing problems," Angel jested, patting his leg. Mom stalked into the living room, holding a glass of wine for Angel.

"Zamari, I know you have work tomorrow, so here's some sweet iced tea," Mom explained, passing him the glass.

"Thanks, Geraldine. How is everything at the church? Angel told me she made a donation on our behalf to the women's shelter," Zamari confirmed, taking a sip of his tea while holding Angel's hand.

"That reminds me. You're all invited to the fundraiser." Angel put her drink on the coffee table, reached into her purse, and removed an envelope.

"Another boring night of having old women hit on me," Caleb groaned, swiping the top of his head.

"Which is why I suggested you bring a date. I mean, Kianna should be your plus one," Angel suggested, crossing her legs.

"Uhm, Kianna never said she was going," I responded.

"Of course, she's going, especially being on the arm of Caleb Glover, the son of the hospital's top doctor," Mom said.

I rolled my eyes and could feel my blood boiling at them for trying to play matchmaker. "Kianna, don't look so down. Caleb is a respectful young guy," Angel teased.

Caleb poked me in the side of my hip, warmth prinked my skin and I turned my head, focusing on the tv with the sports game.

"Are we ready to eat?" Mom suggested.

Jumping up first, I skipped to the dining room ready to get the dinner over with so I could get back to my apartment. Everybody filed in behind me. Caleb took a seat next to me, and my dad was at the head of the table as usual with Mom at his right, with Zamari and Angel across from me and Caleb.

Removing the aluminum foil from the green beans, I passed it to Caleb, then took a piece of baked chicken. Everyone started to indulge in the meal.

"Caleb, are you dating anyone at the moment?" Mom asked.

"Mom," I hissed and gave her the side eye. I never knew where she would take a conversation. A weird nervous rumbling filled my stomach.

"No, ma'am. Too busy with work and dealing with your crazy daughter," Caleb joked, and I slapped him on the arm.

We all laughed and continued to talk about the fundraiser, while Angel gossiped about a few of the women at the hospital flirting with her husband. After saying goodbye to my and Caleb's parents, he drove us back to the apartment. We stepped inside and Caleb locked the door behind him. I headed for my bedroom. I showered and changed into a pair of shorts, large t-shirt, and socks. I headed out of my bedroom and saw Caleb coming out of the kitchen. He kicked off his Nike slides, grabbed the remote, and turned the tv to a movie. Carrying a bowl of popcorn and two bottled waters, I took a seat on the opposite end of the couch from him, then covered my legs with the blanket. Shiva jumped up on the couch, scratching the corner. I reached over to see what she was digging up and shook my head.

"Shiva, what are you doing, little girl?" I talked to her as if she would answer me. Her head whipped around at the sound of my voice and she crawled into my lap. I tugged on the string and saw her little toy was stuck, so I pulled it out to throw it on the ground.

"You're still acting weird, bug." He extended my feet across his legs. I tried to move, and he glared at me and massaged my feet.

"No, I'm not." I darted my eyes from the tv and back to him.

"What do you call it? At dinner, we barely spoke, and you acted like I had the cooties when I touched you just now."

Shiva came back over with the toy in her mouth to play.

"Caleb, everything is not about you, buddy." Right as I tried to take it out of her mouth she swiveled toward Caleb.

"Are you picking favorites, Shiva?"

He scowled. "Bug, we kissed. Do you want to talk about what happened?"

I shrugged. I very much wanted to talk about it, but not with him. An arrogant smile spread across his face and my pussy thumped.

Calm down.

Shiva purred, and I knew she wasn't flirting with my man. *What am I saying? Caleb is not my man.*

The last time I had sex was four months ago after a

concert Kizzie, Raven, and I got tickets for through my job. I'd dated Matt for a year prior and we normally argued then fucked our brains out. He was pissed I went out without him, and coming home to him shirtless on my bed and a little tipsy led to us cursing and sucking on each other.

I went to pet Shiva on top of her head and she hissed at me. "Ohh, you're scandalous." I watched her lick her butt, then crawl up the couch and place her body on top of Caleb's face.

Exhaling, I sat the bowl of popcorn on the table and wiped my hands clean on the napkin. "Friends kiss, Caleb. It's not a big deal," I asserted.

"Friends normally keep the tongue out of a kiss. The way you slipped yours down my throat..." he taunted me and moved Shiva onto his lap.

"Liar. Anyway, I want to focus on the interview."

"Well sorry to tell you, *buddy*, but I'm getting that promotion."

"Please, no one is better equipped for the role than me."

"Want to bet?" he asked. There was twist to his mouth.

"Bet?"

"Yeah. If you get the job, I will leave the kiss alone. Never bring it up again."

"What if you get the job?"

He grinned and rubbed his hands together. "I get to take you out on a real date."

"Huh?" I paused for a breath.

"Seriously, Kianna, you can keep running, but you know deep down, the feelings are mutual."

"Considering your ex, Sharice, is still roaming around, I doubt a date would work."

Shiva ran out of the room at the sound of my raised voice. Caleb hunched his shoulders.

But then the idiot laughed and tickled the bottom of my foot. "Stop, Caleb!" I tried to snatch my foot way. He leaned forward, pulled me on top of his lap, and moved my legs to straddle him.

"I like you, bug. As more than friends, but I never want you to feel like I'm pressuring you."

Looking away from his eyes, I flashed back to that time in college when I confessed to Ava how I really felt about Caleb.

Ava and I left the library after studying for exams. We walked across campus to my dorm room, making it back in time to get dressed for a party.

"He's your best friend, Kianna."

"I'm so anxious around him. No man has ever made me feel alive."

"Do you think he feels the same?" Ava quizzed, shoveling the ice cream in her mouth.

A loud knock on the door stopped me from answering. I turned the knob and almost lost my breath at Caleb's tall frame standing at the entrance with a smirk on his face.

"What up, sleepyhead?" Caleb pinched my cheek and headed to the couch, bypassing my pile of laundry on the floor.

I shut the door behind him. "Ugh, Caleb, what if I had plans tonight with a guy?"

He grumbled under his breath. "He's not stupid, bug." Caleb popped his feet on the table and made himself at home. Ava snickered at him and headed toward her bedroom.

"I don't want to mess up our friendship," I said as I voiced my concerns.

"Then our bet shouldn't hurt anything."

He extended his hand for us to shake and agree. I stared down at his long, thick fingers. "Most men have to earn a date with me."

"I'm not most men." No, he was not.

Shaking his hand, I worried agreeing to the bet would break up a longstanding friendship and hurt our families.

"Can I sit back down now?"

"Why? You don't like being this close to me, bug?"

He clenched both sides of my hip. I tried not to squirm, but I felt his dick poking at me. A hot flash rose through my core.

"I-I need some more water," I stammered. I jumped out of his lap, ran to the kitchen, hearing his boisterous laughter.

Chapter 4

Caleb

I motioned the company truck to back up and helped unload more stands to block off different areas we set up. Every team had to be here bright and early to organize and finalize before the music fans arrived for the festival. Cheston had me on talent duty, while Kianna was in charge of monitoring the number of people coming in and out. Working up close with talent and making sure they had everything in their trailers, plus being the first on call made me feel good. Kianna had a tight lip when Cheston gave out the orders of the day but kept her feelings to herself. I knew making that bet could change things for us, but in my mind it would be for the better. No matter what I wanted her happy. Driving the golf cart from the trailer up to the stage, I let the assistants and hair team get out to continue working with a local rapper in the city named Young Tina who went viral last year off her hit song *Big Bank*. Most of my boys and I thought she reminded us of Lil' Kim with the different color hair and matching outfits. Her flows and tone on each song told a story and brought you into her world.

"That's fire!" a group of men shouted, laughing together, and drew my attention after parking the cart.

"Fuck you, Matt!" Kianna sneered, and it sent a chill down my spine. Hearing her in distress in any type of situation, especially from her ex, pissed me off. I jogged over to the commotion, pushed through the crowd, and saw Kianna trying to grab something from Matt.

Lifting her funnel cake in her hand, she smashed it in his face. The entire crowd laughed, filming on their phones. I watched him clench his fist at his sides, and Kianna must have sensed his embarrassment. Snatching her phone from the ground, she wiped it off on her pants leg and pushed it in her pocket.

"Keep it walking" I growled.

He snarled and took a step forward. "I knew you were fucking him. Spewing that best friend bullshit." Matt scoffed, brushing his clothes off.

I approached and bumped his shoulder. "No, Caleb. I promise he's not worth it, especially here." Kianna looked at me. His harsh stare lingered on her and I knew I had to do something so he would move on. Still, I wasn't sure how she would react. I extended my arm around her neck, cupped her jaw, and kissed her. Softly, just a peck on her lips. Her eyes expanded in surprise. Matt mumbled something under his breath and walked away.

Kianna shoved me away. Her chest heaved up and down as she tried to catch her breath.

"What was that?"

She marched behind me to the golf cart in a hissy fit. "Bug, get back to work. Cheston is watching."

"So? You just kissed me."

"You're welcome." I logged the meal orders. I reached

for my walkie to let them know I was leaving my post, but Kianna grabbed it out of my hands.

"I wasn't saying thank you, jack ass," Kianna hissed and slammed it into my chest. She turned to walk off, but her shoes were untied and got caught on a pile of dog shit, I watched as she slipped head first to the ground.

Chuckling at her freakout, I bent down to help her stand up, but she refused.

"Bug, let me help."

"No, I'm so embarrassed." Kianna kicked off her shoes with so much disgust and tossed them into the trash before she limped to the bathroom. Trailing behind her, I knocked on the door and waited for her to respond.

"Kianna, open the door."

"Leave me alone, Caleb."

"Where the hell is Kianna?" Cheston barked, holding a clipboard in his hand.

"She's getting cleaned up."

He banged on the port-a-potty. "Kianna, why the hell am I hearing you're fighting in the front of the line."

"That wasn't my fault," Kianna yelled through the door,

"You got one more chance before I put you on probation. I have too much riding on this festival. You get back to your station," Cheston fussed at her and then pointed at me.

"Alright! Kianna, are you good?" I took a deep breath.

She spoke breathlessly. "I'm fine."

"See, she's grown and can handle being in the bathroom alone," Cheston chastised.

Going to the food trucks, I put in all four orders for talent, their assistants, and team. While I waited on the food, I listened to the group on stage go into their third song. When the food was ready, I thanked the cook at the food truck and picked up the stack of foam plates.

"Help!"

A familiar scream pierced my ears, and I whipped around to see the port-a-potty being driven away, the same one Kianna went in to get cleaned up.

"Shit! Kianna, hold on," I yelled. I forgot the food in my hand, dropping it on the ground.

"Caleb! Get me out of here!" Kianna shouted, crying.

I ran to catch up with the truck. I tried to grip the side of the door and noticed the latch wasn't opening. "Yo! Stop!" I yelled at the driver. I tugged on the door again but the latch still wouldn't open. I jogged to the front of the truck.

"Caleb! I can't get out!"

"Stop the truck!" I barked at the driver. He stomped on the brakes and rolled the window down.

"Are you crazy, young man?" the older driver shouted.

Ignoring him, I yanked the door open and grabbed the keys out of the ignition. I rushed to the door of the portable and put the key in trying to get it open.

The driver jumped out of the car and ran up on me. "I can have you arrested."

"My friend's stuck in there."

"Help!" Kianna screamed and the sound of her distress caused him to run around and grab some tools to help get the door open.

The driver finally got the door open and Kianna jumped into my arms. I pulled her into my chest. I tried to console her by rubbing her back and hugging her tighter. "Shusshhh...I'm here."

"What the hell is going on? You two should be at your

stations," Cheston screamed as he tapped on his clipboard. His face turned a bright, angry red.

"I got stuck in there." Kianna wiped her tears away.

"Chill, Cheston. She needs a break."

"A break?" Cheston scrunched his nose and glared at us.

Blowing out a breath, Kianna stepped out of my hold. "I'm fine, Caleb. Go back to your area," she mumbled in defeat as she pulled her braids into a ponytail.

"Listen, I will give you the rest of the day off. From the smell coming off you, it seems like you could use a spa day or something." Cheston waved a hand in the air.

I gave her shoulder a comforting squeeze. "I can take you home," I offered.

"No, please go back and finish working. At least one of us can get the job."

Kianna walked away and Cheston turned to go back to the stage, giving out orders. Exhaling a long breath, I headed back to the food truck and reordered all the food I dropped on the ground. Later in the evening, after the last concert ended, we packed up the equipment and were ready to say good night.

"Caleb, we're going up the street to have a few drinks. You down?" Albert, one of the announcers at the station, asked.

I stood at my car with my keys in my hand. I was ready to leave. "I'm good, Albert. Taking it in for the night."

"You sure?" he asked again. He extended his fist out for a bump.

I stretched out to bump his fist and then popped the lock for my car. "I'm exhausted from the day, man, then I got my folks' upcoming charity dinner."

"Good look. What's up with Kianna and Cheston?"

I drew a long, tired breath. "We're both up for the role of Promotions Director and Cheston's not letting up on Kianna."

Albert clapped me on the back. "Cheston's just riding her because she doesn't take his shit."

"For sure. I have to head home and shower before the early interview."

"Good luck, man. Both of you started together as interns. I see the potential."

"Thanks, Albert."

Albert walked away, and I climbed into car. I cranked the engine and turned up my radio. I was glad I left the top down to get some fresh air while I drove home, thinking about today's events. Checking the time, it just hit nine pm, and seeing Sharice's name on my phone, I declined.

The phone rings again with Sharice's number. "Damn, take a hint." I hit decline again, turning at the light and heading toward the freeway. After a short ride, I pulled into the parking lot of one of my favorite late night burger joints. I edged closer to the pickup window to make an order.

"Can I get two double cheeseburger combos and a side of nuggets."

"Your total will be twelve dollars. Please pull up the window," the operator told me. Once I paid, I pulled off and headed down the street and arrived home, parking in the residential section. I grabbed the bags of food and strolled through the lobby. I hopped on the elevator and hit the button for my floor. Turning my phone on silent, I got off on my floor, before turning to my door, and slid the emergency key Kianna gave me since we stayed on the same floor. Glancing around the quiet living room, all the blinds were closed. Kicking off my shoes, I headed to the back to her bedroom and gently knocked.

"It's open, Caleb."

I opened the door to her room and saw a small body curled under the blankets with the tv playing *Real Housewives* on low. I shook my head and placed the food on the nightstand. I took off my jacket and opened a side drawer where I kept a few items in case I stayed over. I changed into sweats and a white shirt, then lifted the covers and motioned for her to move over.

Shiva was a human woman. I could have sworn she swished her hips. By the slowness of her coming into the bedroom I thought she was trying to seduce me.

"This is my side of the bed," Kianna announced.

"Since when? You know I always sleep next to the door."

She groaned and rolled her eyes at me but she scooted to the right, all while cussing me out. I passed the bag of nuggets, fries, and lemonade to her. Before Shiva could get on the bed, Kianna made her sleep in her bed in the corner, and she did not like that rule.

"Thank you," she mumbled.

I leaned over to kiss her on the forehead. "You're welcome, Kianna."

"What?"

"I said you're welcome."

"No, you called me Kianna."

"That is your name, right?"

"I like when you call me bug," she moaned and tossed a fry in her mouth. The low moan had my dick twitching, ready to fuck.

"Shiva looks like she's ready to fight. Earlier you said you hated the nickname I gave you."

"Shiva will live, and can't a girl change her mind?" She raised my arm, snuggled up close, and laid her head on my chest.

"I'm sorry about today."

"Cheston's going to fire me," she said.

"No, he's not."

Kianna looked up at me. "Nothing I do is good enough for him," she said and popped a nugget in her mouth.

I caressed her cheek and stared into her eyes. "Fuck Cheston, Matt, and whoever else puts those thoughts in your head. Remember you're Kianna *bug* Berry." I jested, then she hit me on the arm.

"That is not my middle name, you jerk."

"Well, I like it for you because you be bugging."

Chortling at my playful attitude, we settled in together and I picked up the remote to turn the channel.

"What are you doing?"

"You've watched every season of these shows. The game's on. I want to watch."

"Then go to your place. My place, my rules." She had a tight hold on the remote and of course, I let her have her way again.

"Big baby."

She stuck her tongue out at me. "You and my dad made me like this."

"Right, I feel for the guy that ends up marrying you," I grunted, setting the alarm clock to get up a little earlier and head to my place to shower and change for work.

"He's going to know you and Daddy set the standards for how I want to be treated." She looked away and I just stared at her side profile, smiling at her confession of knowing her worth and never settling for less than.

"Good night, bug."

"Night, *best friend*," she replied.

Shiva purred.

Chapter 5

Caleb

L ast time my father had one of these fundraising events I avoided them for the entire month, pretending to be sick for a week, taking extra shifts at the station, or going out of town. After my mom got tired of me screening her calls, she'd get my aunt and my grandparents to try and force me to come. It was always about showcasing my father's legacy. It wasn't my type of vibe to pretend around these fake folks. The men either wanted to act like their balls were bigger by bragging of their wealth, or the women would constantly flirt with me. My mom often introduced me as her single son looking for a wife, and I would end up in weird conversations with women of all ages, flirting all night. Tonight I had my boys and Kianna with me to help the time go by quicker. "What's the point of this party, anyway?" Lamar inquired and grabbed the shot of Hennessy off the bar.

"The hospital is raising money for cancer research, plus I found out the radio station is one of the sponsors and that will help me get in more time with the bosses." I adjusted my cufflinks.

"I hope they have some good food tonight. I've already scooped out a few ladies I might hit up," Lamar said. I had invited my best friends, Lamar and Oscar, but I was regretting bringing him because he'd already tried to pick up two women, and one was married. The older woman was one of my father's colleagues, Doctor Rebecca—a short, dark brown skinned woman with a pixie cut and streaks of gray. She had to be in her late fifties, but Lamar never cared as long as he could get food and pussy out of a woman. Ava and Blaze showed up for a surprise visit from out of town, so I extended an invitation after they spent Sunday dinner at Kianna's parents' house. Before Ava moved to be with Blaze officially, he'd hung out with me and the guys a few times.

"Probably. The question is do they want you?" I joked. Lamar flipped me off.

"Fuck you, Caleb," Lamar jested. "We know your eyes only stay on one person."

"Have you made the move yet?" Blaze pointed at Kianna laughing with Ava and my mom. The party's held in a fancy ballroom they rented for tonight.

"I don't know who you are talking about." I thanked the bartender and slid a tip onto the counter.

"She must have turned you down." Blaze smirked, gulping the rest of his drink, and motioned for another order.

He was pretty cool for a guy with a million-dollar business, but if he became another Lamar and got in my business on the Kianna situation, we would have problems. Think Blaze would know how the Johnson cousins were since he had to go through a lot with Ava constantly running from him. After a few rounds of basketball and beating his ass on the court he fit right in with my group of friends.

"Ava must have gotten your ass in check before coming here since you've stayed glued to her all night." Music blasted as people danced in the middle of the floor. Most of these events were boring with speeches, but I was serious about the position at the station so I had to show up. The owner was adamant about being a team player, having the crew demonstrate their savviness in tough situations. Kissing ass wasn't my strong suit, but becoming a promoter with pay was the goal.

"There's your future coming this way." Lamar nudged me, and I glanced around. I saw Kianna, Ava, and their other friend, Trisha, were headed our way.

I narrowed my eyes. "Not tonight, Lamar." I patted him on the chest to be cool. He and Trisha were hell together.

"Gentlemen, don't you look sharp tonight? Even you, Lamar," Trisha teased, linking her arm with Ava's.

"The wicked witch of the south. How did I get the pleasure?" Lamar responded, bowing his head.

"Fuck you, Lamar, with your short ass," Trisha hissed.

"B—" Lamar started to curse. I stretched my arm around his shoulder and turned him away from her.

"That's right, run away, little boy," Trisha taunted, and Ava tapped her on the shoulder to shut up.

"What? He started it with me!" Trisha fussed. Her lips formed into a pout.

"Trisha, normally I would agree, but Lamar really was trying to be nice," Kianna claimed.

"Whose side are you, Kianna?" Trisha demanded and cocked her head to the side.

"Girl, I'm here to enjoy the free food, drinks, and have

fun," Kianna answered before she bit into a shrimp roll and wiping away the sauce with a napkin.

"Caleb, I hear you're going for the same position as Kianna. Are you nervous?" Ava probed. Blaze came up beside her, clasping his arm around her waist.

"Ava, I told you that in confidence," Kianna huffed, then rolled her eyes at her cousin.

"Kianna and I started at the same time. Cheston, our boss, is making it a little harder for the both of us, but I'm confident I can get the job."

"I know you two love working in the music business," Ava exclaimed as we all made our way over to our assigned table as the speeches started.

"Here we go. Cheston's already making the night exhausting." Kianna put on a fake smile because Cheston was approaching our table.

"Kianna, Caleb, I need you two to get the line organized. One of the other staff members called out," Cheston informed us.

"We're guests tonight, Cheston," Kianna complained, scooting back from the table.

"Are you not ready for the responsibility of promotions director because I have a list of people ready and willing," Cheston challenged. Before Kianna could give a slick comeback, I stepped in to halt the argument.

"It's all good, Cheston. We can handle the line management."

"Great. See, Kianna, if you were more like Caleb, you'd be higher on the list for an interview," Cheston criticized her, handing me a list of names for the door, and stalked off back to the corner of the room where radio station DJs were doing interviews.

"I hate him," Kianna grunted and snatched the second list out of my hand.

"Come on, bug. We can knock this out in no time."

"He's right, Kianna. Your bosses are watching," Ava emphasized.

I saw my parents waving at me. I led Kianna forward. Taking the left side, I headed to the front, and she headed to the right near a roped off area. Her side had one of the longest lines for entry to the event. By scanning each ticket, marking off names, and thanking each guest for attending, I helped keep the crowd moving.

As soon as I felt things would be smooth sailing, my stomach sank at Sharice switching places. She came over to my line wearing a smug grin with a guy on her arm.

"Name." I kept my eye contact steady, not letting her attempts at jealousy get to me.

"Robert Mason and guest." The preppy guy she had swindled into bringing her smiled brightly.

"Go ahead." To keep her from talking to me, I rushed them through and handed the list to another team member and walked back in to find my parents.

"Hey, baby, having fun?" Mom checked and ran a hand down my cheek.

"Fun is an understatement."

"Oh, hush. You look so cute in your suit," Mom bragged, turning me around to show me off.

"All right, old woman."

"I got your old woman. Anyway, where's Kianna? I thought she was just with you."

"She's working the front door."

"Hopefully you two will be able to enjoy yourselves and not work all night," Mom said in a raised angry voice, giving Cheston a glare as he waved back with a smile.

Chuckling at her demeanor, I leaned down to kiss her cheek and went back to the table with my friends. "Where's Kianna?" Ava asked.

"She's probably still working the line."

"Hello, would anyone like shrimp rolls?" the server offered. I took a few off her hands. I popped one in my mouth while the announcer read off each donation and thanked the donors.

"I just got the numbers of two women, and one is going through a divorce," Lamar announced gleefully, standing next to the table.

"Son!" my mom shouted in distress as she ran to our section.

"What's wrong?"

Mom gestured to the hallway. "Kianna needs your help."

"What happened?" I asked urgently. Everyone hopped up in a panic. I rushed down the hall, not finding Kianna, only seeing Sharice yelling.

I pushed through the crowd surrounding Sharice. "Where is she?"

"Fuck you and Caleb. Robert is ten times better," Sharice spewed more hate.

"Sharice, back up." I moved around two other girls who were laughing in the corner at the fight. Having her act crazy at my parents' event only pissed me off more.

"Caleb, tell this girl I am not the one." Kianna balled up her fist, reaching around me to hit Sharice. I grabbed her in a bear hug and moved her away even as she tried to reach around me again to land a hit on Sharice.

"Watch out!" Kianna screamed from behind me. I whipped around to see Cheston charge in like a raging bull. I knew then that my chances of getting the job were diminishing.

"Jesus, please cover and grant them some solitude," Geraldine blurted, raising her hands in prayer.

All eyes moved to her, and I felt Kianna stiffen in my arms. "Calm down, bug."

"She started it." Kianna clawed her way out of my hold.

"I should have known you had something to do with a fight at one of the most important events for the city," Cheston accused Kianna..

Geraldine glared at him. "Who are you to talk to my daughter like that?"

"Oh god." Kianna tried to step in between her mother and Cheston.

"Excuse me?" Cheston replied.

"Ma, this is my boss. Stay out of it please," Kianna begged her mother and shook her head.

"No, he needs to apologize," Geraldine commanded.

"That's not happening and as a matter of fact, you are on documented coaching." Cheston lifted his clipboard, making notes. Kianna's mouth hung open, then closed, and tears streamed down her face.

Laughter came from the same group of girls, and it sent a sting to my heart. I knew Kianna hated being embarrassed, especially in front of her mother.

"I apologize, Cheston. It won't happen again," Kianna responded, took the warning, and walked back to sit down.

The hallway cleared out a few seconds later and I headed to check on Kianna, with her mother beside me.

"Kianna, are you alright?"

"Honey, you don't need that job." Geraldine's voice shook with fury.

"Actually, I'm ready to leave. It's been a long day. Do you mind taking me home?" Kianna asked, and I nodded.

"Are you sure you want to be alone? How about coming to the house with me and your father?" Geraldine pleaded.

She gave her mom a hug. "I will call you tomorrow. I promise I'm fine. Cheston's all bark and no bite," she giggled.

We left the banquet hall, and I handed my ticket to the valet to bring my car around. Both guys had weird looks on their faces.

"Where's my car?"

"Sir, there was an accident," he informed me.

"What kind of an accident?"

He motioned to the parking lot. I glanced over his shoulder and my eyes widened in surprise at my car being totaled—from all the windows being busted, to the writing on the side of the door that labeled me a *cheater*.

"You know Sharice did it, right?" Kianna grimaced and pulled out her phone.

"She's paying to fix my car."

"That's your crazy ex," Kianna said. "A ride share is coming."

"Thanks." I checked the damages and made a call to my father to get a tow truck to pick up my car and taken to the shop he uses.

* * *

After my workout, I took a quick shower and got food cooking. I turned my phone on do not disturb and planned to relax the entire weekend after the charity event ended in disaster. Luckily my father and the hospital raised over fifty thousand dollars, which helped to overshadow Sharice's tactics for getting under my skin. I turned the volumes up on the basketball game, popped the lid on my beer, and took a gulp. The smell of the ravioli, baked salmon, and cheesecake in the oven had my stomach growling.

Bang! Bang!

"Caleb!" Kianna screamed, and I hopped up and rushed to the door. I yanked it open, seeing her drenched clothes and her face covered with tears.

"What happened?"

"I need your help. My apartment is flooding!" Kianna passed Shiva to me, then ran across the hall. I trailed behind to the door, shocked at seeing the entire floor covered with water.

I put Shiva down and I sprinted out the door, forgetting to put on shoes. My arms went up suddenly, my feet lost control, and then my ass hit the floor.

"Fuck!" I grunted, holding my elbow from the pain.

"Caleb, what are you doing?"

"Bug, I fell."

"Duh, get up and help me!" Kianna extended a hand to pull me up. I sluiced through the water, trying to get a steady footing. But I fell back down, bringing her with me.

"Caleb, this is not play time."

I couldn't help it. I burst into laughter, staring at her poked out lips. Her golden braids were half hanging out of the ponytail, and her t-shirt and shorts were soaked. Feeling the rumbling of my laughter, she fell over onto her back, chuckling next to me.

"What the hell are you doing?"

We slowly sat up at the sound of voices. The shuffling of feet came into view as another tenant and the maintenance manager came to help.

"I heard you screaming and called Joey," Lily, the older tenant down the hall, said.

"Thanks. I'm so sorry to bother you." Kianna stood, and I tightened the string on my pants as I stood up. Joey came in and stopped the water. Scanning all the damage, he scratched his head.

"How did this happen?"

"It's a long story," Kianna told him.

"You will need to stay somewhere else until we can get things cleaned up," Joey explained.

Kianna whimpered, tossed her head back, and closed her eyes in annoyance. "My parents are going to kill me."

"Come on. You can't do anything right now. Get some clothes and come shower at my place."

"I can't impose on you, Caleb."

"Either my place or your parents'."

"Right, Geraldine will have me up at the crack of dawn every day," Kianna muttered and sauntered toward her bedroom.

"How bad is it really?" I probed.

"At least a few weeks to get it completely dried out, cleaned, and repainted." Joey released a heavy breath and put away his tools.

"Damn."

Kianna's apartment damage would probably end up costing her more than she wanted and she would have to ask for help from her parents. As her friend I would have her back, especially with her still having problems at work.

Chapter 6

Kianna

I was dancing around my apartment, listening to the *Renaissance* album by Beyonce. I rocked my hips side to side and poured peppermint bubble soap in my bath water. Since Cheston put me on a documented coaching, I had to be extra pleasant and not show how much I hated him. Since I had the day off, I planned on pampering myself with a bubble bath, red wine, and great music. I threw the empty bottle in the trash and pinned my hair up on top of my head. I snapped my fingers to go check on the food I just ordered when the doorbell rang. Shiva stared back at me and turned her head to the open window blinds.

"She's no fun," I murmured.

I rushed out of the bathroom and rushed to the door.

"Kianna Berry?" the delivery driver asked.

"That's me."

He passed me the bags of food. I thanked him and kicked the door closed with my foot. I skipped to the kitchen, grabbing plate and fork on my way to the bar. I grabbed some wine from the fridge and filled my glass to *the rim. I sat down on the stool, opened my dinner, and tasted the first bite of smothered steak and red rice. I closed my eyes and moaned with delight.*

"So good."

My cell phone rang and I picked it up to see Ava was calling. I laughed out loud. She had sent a text earlier telling me to answer my phone. I'd avoided most of my friends from the dinner because I was too embarrassed.

Shiva crawled into my lap as I answered the phone. "Yes, cousin."

"Why did I get ignored?" Ava sassed.

"Cousin, I'm sorry."

"Whatever."

"Don't be mean."

"Mean is you, for ignoring your family."

"My mom must have called you." I climbed off the stool but was startled when I felt water under my feet. Then I watched in horror as a pile of my books floated into the kitchen.

"My books!"

"Kianna?" Ava called my name. I dropped my phone and ran out of the kitchen, I almost tripped so I held onto the wall.

"Kianna! What happened?" Ava shouted. I rushed to the bathroom, and the entire bathroom was filled with water up to my ankle.

"I left the water on in the bathroom and now it's flooded." Jogging to the door, wrapping a hand around the knob, it wouldn't open.

"Got damn it. It's stuck!" Shiva ran to jump on the top window sill. I ran to get her in her crate and busted my ass.

"Do you need me to come over there?"

I shoved my shoulder into the door. I pried it open,

then slipped and fell in the water, dropping my phone. "Of course, my phone slips out of my hand," I muttered to myself. I crawled to the tub and reached for the knob to turn it off. Nothing happened.

"Please don't be stuck."

"Kianna!" Caleb's voice brought me out of the flashback of my apartment flooding. Holding a heating pad to my tail bone, I was laid across the couch in fresh pair of shorts and one of his large shirts.

"You hungry, bug?"

"No."

"Come on, Kianna. It's not the end of the world." Caleb came to sit on the opposite side of his couch. I raised my eyes up to his face, seeing those big brown eyes stare back at me. Caleb was always able to cheer me up in any situation, and the only things that would cheer me up were alcohol or sex and asking him for the latter would be foolish.

He snapped his hands in front of my face.

"Huh?"

"Where did you go?"

"Just thinking."

"About?"

"Life."

"Come on, stop being depressed. Joey said it would be a few weeks, and your place will be back to brand new."

Slouching down in the couch, I pulled my legs up to my chest. "I really hate to move back in with my parents."

"Stay here," he said nonchalantly with hunched shoulders.

"No."

"Why not?"

"Caleb, it's your apartment. I would feel bad invading your space. What if you bring a girl back here?"

"Stop playing with me, bug." Grasping a hold of my legs, he propped them on top of his lap.

I held the side of my head with my arm and watched him massage my feet. "You know I snore, need my alone time, and hate people that eat my food." I ran a list of my grievances to see his reaction, and the jerk just laughed at me.

Caleb spoke in an amused tone. "Kianna, how long have we known each other?"

"Too damn long." I kept my voice steady, then lifted my hair to put in a ponytail.

He took my hand. "Exactly. Too damn long. Hell, at least over five years. Nothing surprises me anymore."

"Okay, I get your point, jerk."

His voice softened. "Stay here and relax."

"Cheston wants to see us on Monday."

"How are you feeling about the interview?" Caleb watched Shiva tear up his shoes.

"Honestly, I already know he's going to give you the job." I cocked my head to the side and held up my right hand at the look on his face.

"Stop putting out those bad vibes. You owe me a new pair of shoes."

"That's her love language. We will see on Monday."

"We will, so let's get dressed."

"Why?"

"I want to go out."

"Why not stay here and help me drink my sorrows away?" I whined, pulling the blanket on the couch over my head.

"Because you might set my place on fire next," Caleb

joked. I felt myself being lifted off the couch, the blanket snatched away, then being and thrown over his shoulders.

"Caleb, put me down."

Smack!

"Ouch, asshole!" *Shiva needs to tear all of his shoes up,* I thought to myself.

He chuckled as he walked us back to the bedrooms to get dressed. Thirty minutes later we walked along the park with ice cream. It was a nice Saturday in Boston— not too hot, not too cold, with a great breeze in the air.

"How are you feeling now, bug?"

Swiping some of the ice cream off my hand, I told him, "Better, so thanks for bringing me out here."

"See, listening to me works out great."

Taking a deep breath, I wrinkled my nose. "Sure, Caleb."

"Let's take a seat on the bench."

"I want to bike ride, so come on."

"Why are you avoiding this conversation, Kianna?"

"What conversation?"

Caleb fixed his eyes on my face. "You and me."

"Caleb, the ice cream is going to your head." I giggled.

"Nope, we made a bet and I plan on sticking to my end of the bargain."

I shooed him away. "Some girl filled your head up. Getting too cocky."

Caleb stepped in front of me, opened his mouth, and took the entire top of the ice cream scoop out of my hand.

"Seriously!" I tossed the rest in the trash and flipped him off.

He chortled, wiping his mouth clean with the napkin. "Never doubt me, Kiki."

"*Never doubt me, Kiki,*" I mumbled under my breath.

Paying for the bikes, I climbed on, pushed my hair behind my ear, and followed Caleb through the park. Speeding up to leave him, I moved around a group of kids running in a circle, and their parents were fussing.

I picked up the pace. I whipped my head around and yelled, "Keep up, asshole!"

"Kianna, watch out!"

I quickly turned forward and my eyes widened in horror seeing a large pile of balloons on the ground for a photo shoot. Before I could turn fully with my high speed, I crashed into the balloons.

"Oh my god! What did you do?" a woman standing in front of me shouted. Slowly, I turned on my side, bent my knees, and made sure I hadn't broken any bones.

"Sorry, I couldn't stop in time."

"Kianna, you good?" Caleb approached, helping me to stand.

"I'm fine."

"Who is going to blow up these balloons?" she snapped, and I glanced at the mess I left.

I threw up my hands, knowing our bike ride was over. Caleb nodded and we helped her with the setup for the shoot. After an hour or two, we made it back to Caleb's place.

* * *

Cheston sat back in his chair, ready to throw everything at me during the interview. "Kianna, tell me why you would be a good fit for the job?"

"I feel I would be a great fit for the role because of the amount of years I put in from team building and working on listeners' experiences at different concerts."

He took notes. *Maybe that's a good sign.*

I was so nervous I came in thirty minutes before my appointment to run through mock interviews with one of the other girls who worked at the station and had my back. Adina was around my age and had moved out here a few years ago looking to be an on-air personality.

"The role calls for long hours, sometimes meetings at the drop of a hat. Are you ready for that type of responsibility?"

"I am. Even during certain moments in college, I would help set in certain programs for the students and I wanted to bring that same style here."

"Your relationship status?"

"Relationship?"

"You and Caleb."

"What does Caleb have to do with me?"

"Aren't you two dating? We may not have a policy but dating coworkers can get tricky."

"Did you ask any other employee these questions?"

"I beg your pardon?"

"Cheston, what is the real issue between you and I?"

Taking his glasses off, clasping his hands together, he leaned over the table. "I think you're spoiled and expect to be handed the job."

"That's not true."

"Well, you come in late often, act a fool at functions, and constantly put the station in a bad light on social media."

"And what caused those things?"

"What do you mean?"

"Something had to cause me to act a fool or did you not see that girl get in my face? Plus, I often defend the station on social media and me being late was one time, maybe two when my car broke down." I ran off explanations I knew might not work, but I had to save any chance of getting the job.

"Nice try."

"Come on, Cheston. We both know I would kill it as the Promotions Director. Give me a chance."

"I need to talk with the other candidates and my boss." Cheston stood, picking up his paperwork.

"Thank you for the opportunity." I left the conference room and went back to my cubicle. I plopped down in my chair and logged into my computer.

"How did it go?" Adina asked as she approached from across the room.

"Terrible, he hates me," I told her with defeat in my voice. I dropped my head on the desk.

"He has to look at things objectively even if he hates you," Adina responded. I knew she was trying to cheer me up, but I couldn't do anything but laugh at her statement.

"What's funny?"

"You."

She chuckled. "What'd I say?"

I laughed so hard I felt tears in my eyes. "He hates me but has no choice but to interview me."

"Girl, you a mess."

"Thanks, Adina."

"You're welcome. A few of us are going to lunch together. You down?"

Caleb walked past my desk and winked as he headed inside Cheston's office. I agreed to lunch with Adina, then I picked up my purse and followed her to the elevator. "I could eat after a hellish weekend."

"Yeah, I remember you saying earlier how your place flooded."

I stroked a hand through my braids. "The bathtub flooded over and got everywhere."

My ringing phone disrupted our conversation. I took it out, sauntering off the elevator at the lobby, and caught up with a few more co-workers.

"Hey, Mom."

"How did the interview go?"

I moved my phone from my ear in shock. "Hello?"

"Kianna, stop playing with me," Mom chastised.

I spoke through pursed lips. "You never call and ask about work."

"Trying something new."

I held a hand over the speaker of my cell and asked her quietly, "Are you drinking?"

The silence on the line had me thinking I was right. It was taking too long for her to answer me. She really had been drinking.

"Kianna, don't make me come up there and whack you over the head."

"There's my mother," I snickered, fucking with her.

"Child of mine. Anyway, anything new yet?"

I slid in the car with Adina and two other co-workers. I shut the door and put my seatbelt on. I could hear Dad and Mom bickering back and forth. "Hi Dad."

"Hi bug! Your mom said you got fired."

A flicker of irritation turned into shockwaves of disbelief. "What!"

"She said—" Dad started to speak.

"Titus, I did not say that!" Mom shouted, huffing in the background. My parents loved each other deeply, but at the same time both could push each other's buttons. The amount of times I saw the back and forth growing up, I already knew my dad would always give in to my mom. Mainly because she had to be right in every situation.

"Well, what the hell are you talking about saying she was fired up?" Dad grumbled.

Both of them were so loud, their voices and arguing filled the car and everybody tried to hide their smirking at my parents' craziness.

"I had a job interview, Dad."

"Oh," he answered.

"Give me the phone, Titus," Mom fussed.

"Sweetpea, come see your old man. I might be able to find you a job."

"Dad, I—" Not wanting to deal with their arguing I hung up and pushed the phone back into my purse.

"Your mom and dad are funny," Adina tittered.

My cheeks burned with embarrassment. "Try growing up with them."

I pressed my lips together before I said anything else. I took my phone back out and tapped my message group chat for Ava and Trisha.

Me: Did either of you tell my mom I had the interview today?

Ava: N.

Trisha: Bitch, when did I talk to your parents?

Me: Right, sorry Trisha.

Ava: What happened now?

Me: Geraldine as usual got Dad worked up and said I was fired.

Trisha: Did you?

Me: Did I what?

Trisha: Get fired, dummy.

Me: Shut up Trisha before I block you.

Ava: The interview went good?

Trisha: Probably not if she's messaging us during work hours.

Me: Heffa, it's my lunch time.

Trisha: Oh, bring me something.

Ava: Shut up, Trisha.

Trisha: Yo, Trisha can't come to the phone right now.

Me: Who is this?

Trisha: She's sitting on my dick, call back later.

Ava: TRISHA

Trisha: That was Lamar's dumb ass. He snatched my phone.

Me: Since when are you dating Caleb's best friend?

I had so many questions and a girls' night needed to happen immediately. We parked at the shop I usually ate at with Caleb, turned off the car, and climbed out. When we got in, the waitress sat us at a booth in the back and I waited for Trisha to answer back.

"Order me a club sandwich I have to use the restroom," I told Adina, scooting out of the booth. On my way to the back I dialed Ava's number.

"Girl, what the hell was that with Trisha?" Ava asked without waiting for a hello.

"She's your friend."

"Let me call her on three-way."

I waited for her call to go through and my phone beeped. Caleb called back to back. "Ava, let me call you back. It's Caleb on my other line."

"Hurry up. I fly back to CA in two days," Ava replied.

I swiped over to the other line and answered. "Caleb."

"Bug, you at lunch?" he inquired.

I felt a tinge of heat at him checking in on me. "Yes, I am."

"Usual spot?"

At first I thought it would be a nice conversation, but the dryness in his tone made me rethink if he was okay. "I am, Why?"

"We need to talk."

"You sound mad."

"Wait there," Caleb told me.

"Caleb, is something wrong?"

"Don't leave," Caleb demanded.

Chapter 7

Caleb

I could admit I never expected anything when I applied for the job, especially with Cheston running the station. So many times he'd denied a few of us an opportunity to move up in the workplace and to hear what he thought of me really shocked me. I glanced at Kianna standing at the front of the restaurant staring back at me. The past few days, having her in my apartment felt like it was meant to be between us.

"Caleb, you okay?" Kianna asked when she made it to the door of my Jeep.

"Get in, Kianna."

"Why do I feel like something is wrong?"

I scratched the back of my neck. She knew something was up. I watched her come around to jump inside.

"Tell me."

"I had the interview."

"And?"

"Cheston offered me a job."

Putting on a front, she smiled through her disappointment and I hated how much more I would hurt her.

"Congrats! You've always wanted the position, plus I owe you a date," she giggled.

"It's a job in another state."

"Wait! You mean a promoter job in another state?"

Weaving through traffic, I hopped on the freeway and headed home. "He's offering you the position here."

Her mouth fell open, and her eyes widened in shock and disbelief. "How? I mean—When?"

"Cheston told me not to say anything, but as your best friend, I wanted to talk with you first."

"You're taking the job! What is there to talk about?"

Finally making it home, I parked. "I mean…"

"Caleb, shut up. We both wanted these jobs, so giving it up now would be foolish."

Reaching in the backseat, I grabbed the food I picked up before I called her after Cheston said we could have the rest of the day off.

"Why are we back home? Cheston's going to kill me." She started to panic, but I pulled her into my chest and crushed my lips to hers.

"Mmmmmm…Caleb." She moaned and gently moved out of my grasp.

"Cheston should be calling you in about five."

Right as I counted down, her phone rang and she answered. She was spooked at first and stumbled and I helped her.

Pushing through the lobby door, I headed toward elevator. Kianna trailed next to me. "Hey Cheston."

I pressed the button for our floor.

"Uhh, yes, I do. I know. Thank you." Kianna excitedly jumped into my arms.

"Congrats, bug."

"He said I have the job and don't fuck it up," Kianna snickered.

"True."

She smacked me on the chest. "Shut up. Anyway, what are you going to do?"

"I have no clue."

We stepped up to my door after getting off the elevator on our floor. I slipped the key in my door and let her walk inside first. "Take the job," she insisted.

I placed the food on the island, then took off my coat and laid it across the couch. "It's in New York."

"That can be fun. We can travel back and forth to see each other."

"You'd do that?"

"Come on, Caleb. You're my best friend."

I pushed her salad in front of her. She took a seat, and I stalked to the fridge and grabbed two sodas.

"I forgot to tell you some gossip."

"Which friend this time got caught up, pregnant, keyed his car, or my favorite—pretended to be a wife and called up to the job to get him fired?"

Cackling at my comments, Kianna slapped her hand on the counter. "Trisha is fucking Lamar."

"That's nothing new."

"Hold up. You knew they were dating?"

"Dating is a strong word."

She gasped. "Fuck buddies?"

I nodded, taking a bite out of my burger. "For at least the last six months."

"That hussy lied to us."

"That is her business."

Her brows knitted together. "Lamar's a playboy."

"Worry about me and you."

Ignoring my statement, she reached to take some of my fries. "What are you talking about, Caleb?"

"You owe me a date."

"How? The bet was about one of us getting a job. We both got jobs."

"Exactly. We both came out winners, so you owe me a date and I owe you."

She smacked her teeth. "Technically, I won."

"Nope, we both came out winners." I drank the rest of the bottled soda and took a bite of my sandwich.

"Okay, you win. To shut you up, I will go on a date."

I pecked her lips, cleaned up my mess, and walked around the island. I stood behind her and nuzzled my head in her neck.

"Caleb."

"Hmmmm..." I smelled her sweet perfume.

"Are you sure?" She cupped the back of my head.

"More than you know."

"My part of the bet dealt with never bringing up the kiss." Kianna rose off the stool. She folded her arms across her chest.

"You won your bet. We will never talk about that one kiss."

"Slick, Mr. Caleb."

I licked my lips and extended my hands to pull her closer. "There will be more kisses we can talk about after the date."

"I feel tricked."

"Hate the game, not the player, baby." I grinned. But she scoffed and tried to push me away. I stumbled a little, but I still held her close.

"Where is the date going to be?"

"A surprise."

"Tell me at least what to wear."

"Something sexy, but comfortable."

"Not much to go on, Caleb." She sauntered to the guest bedroom. I cleaned up the rest of the trash and planned on showing Kianna a good time tonight.

* * *

Surprising Kianna was the goal, and making our first date one to remember was hard because she'd never had a problem with being spoiled by me. For the first time I was kind of nervous where things would go if she hated the idea of being with me officially. First sto,p I had a little unexpected trip planned. Listening to her fuss about the blindfold, I let her ramble on, walking her through the grass.

"Caleb, if you don't tell me where we are, I promise I'm kicking your ass," Kianna spat.

"Okay, bug. You can remove the blindfold."

She opened her eyes, clenching a hand to her chest. "A balloon ride?"

"I figured we can do it a little different."

"Caleb, I never expected you'd remember me telling you one of my fantasies."

Back in college we talked about the different date ideas she'd love a guy to plan. I loved having those memories in my mind and tonight I would try to show her I was serious about us being more than friends.

"Come on. We got it for two hours." I helped her get in without showing off her goodies. Kianna could wear a trash bag and make it look sexy, but she was wearing simple leggings, a crop top, and knee high boots. She had my mouth watering at her plump ass poking out.

I massaged her shoulders and pressed a kiss to her forehead, watching us slowly lift off the ground. She wrapped her arms around my waist and laid her head on my chest, while I ran a hand up and down her back.

"So beautiful out here."

"The beauty is in front of me right now."

"And he's charming too." She stood on her toes to kiss me. Kianna shoved her hand in her pocket. I watched her take her phone and snap pictures of the scenery and us together. Seeing the smile on her face and the joy in her expression brought a warm feeling to my heart. She was happy.

Once our balloon ride finished, we had worked up a hunger. So, I brought her to her next favorite idea of a date, dinner on a boat ride. Pulling on some of my father's connections, I got to rent a luxury boat for a low cost, with the promise to give the guy free tickets for his teen daughters for six months.

"Caleb, you have outdid yourself."

"Come on, I told you to give me a chance."

"Dinner on a boat."

"Another item checked off your list." I helped her onto the boat and took her jacket, while the crew handed us glasses of champagne.

"Am I doing good so far?"

"Beyond my dreams, I have to admit to myself. Deep down I have wanted you but fought those feelings."

"I understood not wanting to break our friendship."

A somber look glazed over her face. "I'm glad you persisted."

"Me, too, but why do you look sad?"

"You're going to leave for another job."

"We don't need to think about that right now."

"Long distance is going to be hard."

Caressing her palm, I lifted her hand to my lips, placing a kiss on top. "Eat."

"First, Trisha and Lamar. Now, me and you," she remembered, polishing off her salmon.

"Trisha and Lamar have nothing on what we're building."

"I'm gonna hold you to that." She wiped her mouth. We laughed at them going back and forth the other day on the phone. The crew picked up our dishes, refilled our glasses, then handed us a slice of chocolate mousse, her favorite dessert.

"What do you think your mom will say?"

"Probably ask me if you've been saved," Kianna joked. I lifted the fork to feed her some of the mouse.

"Momma Geraldine is a hoot."

"She drives me crazy, but I love her."

"Come dance with me."

"There's no music."

Right as she made that comment, Anita Baker filled our ears and the shocked look on Kianna's face sent a shock to my dick.

"Anita Baker."

"Another favorite on your list."

Kianna jumped into my arms, crying. She smashed her lips to mine, sucking on my tongue, while Anita continued to play. I shifted Kianna around in my arms and we glided around the deck in our own world as her favorite artist sung to us.

Chapter 8

Kianna

I turned my head away from him because I knew my blushing at just the touch of his hands would show how much the picture of us together making deep, passionate love would show in my expression. All through college I watched him go out on dates with girls and wished it was me. Caleb awakened a deep desire with his hypnotizing stare. My skin tingled under his fingertips. All of my surrender at not wanting to mess up our friendship went out the window the moment he trailed kisses down my stomach, his hands cupping my breasts. His tall physique hovered over my short body. He ran his tongue across my bottom lip, slowly sliding his tongue into my mouth. I could feel myself losing control and wetting the sheets as our tongues locked together. I pushed my arms up his back, spread my legs farther apart, and gasped when the head of his dick pressed at the entrance of my pussy.

"Caleb, I feel you."

"Baby, I dreamed of this moment."

"I know. Please don't stop."

He thrusted with a shiver of vivid recollection, catching my screams of his name on the tip of my tongue. Skin to skin, as one, he took my hand and guided it to his heart. Our discarded clothes were left along the trail to the bedroom of the boat. After Anita finished, I couldn't even wait long enough to get to his apartment. I managed to not embarrass myself in front of the crew when his hand slid down into my leggings, caressing my clit. Caleb's exploration landed us on a roller coaster ride as he tweaked my nipples. His hands dove down the soft lines of my arms, waist, and hips.

I softly moaned at the firmness of his dick. "Sooooo... Deep," I cooed, encouraged him to give me more.

Stroking his back, this urgency—this neediness I felt—was new to me. *I was in love with my best friend.* My thoughts spun around in my head. My emotions whirled as I wondered how we'd navigate going from friends to lovers. But his touch transported my worries into a cloud of just me and him.

His deep moans engulfed the room. "Fucking drive me crazy, bug, holding out this good pussy."

"Too intense, never felt this before...Yesss," I hissed, arching my back off the bed. The dominating nature of his thrusts, compounded by our heady stares, sent me over the moon into another realm.

Taking my right nipple into his mouth, his hands crawled down to grip my thighs, then expanded them further to open up even deeper. Caleb knew exactly how to make me fall apart, sucking and biting along my shoulder and up to my neck. Having sex with Matt months ago was nothing compared to what I was experiencing with him.

"Hell, yes...bug. I knew it would feel this good," Caleb growled and gazed into my eyes.

I raised my hands to grip both sides of his beautiful face. I captured his lips in a soul shattering kiss.

"Just keep going. I'm coming, baby," I panted, closing my eyes tight.

He sped up his strokes. "Right here, Kianna."

I nodded and thrashed my head as the deep pull of the orgasm settled in my core. His own orgasm overtook him, and then he slowly released. Caleb coming was the last trigger I needed.

Hooking my arm around his neck tight, I came so hard, it felt like the room was spinning and my heart leapt out of my chest.

"Caleb...Yesss!" I screamed. I felt myself arch off the bed and fall back down into the mattress. I snuggled up close to him to catch my breath.

"Damn Kianna, you got my heart, girl," Caleb groaned, peppering kisses to my cheek, forehead as we fell asleep together.

* * *

The next day Caleb had to go to the radio station early. He left a note that said he'd see me later and to not let Brunhilda mess up his place. I chuckled at him going at Shiva again, but my baby was a diva and never shit where she laid her head. The only person running things was her, if you really must know. After vacuuming the carpet I finished off some emails and waited for the food I ordered to get delivered.

"Hello."

"We're here, old lady," Trisha remarked.

"I got your old lady." I ignored her comment, standing up to walk to the door. Swinging it open, Trisha, Kizzie, and Raven stood with bottles in their hands.

Stepping to the side, I waved for them to come in and take a seat. "Where's the food?" Trisha asked.

"Calm down, greedy ass."

"She's been grouchy ever since Lamar called her," Kizzie snitched, and Trisha rolled her eyes at us.

"Oops, love birds fighting again."

"Lamar is not my man," Trisha sassed.

"He's something," Raven cackled.

"Fuck y'all." Trisha slouched down in the loveseat.

Taking out some cups, I headed into the living room and helped to open the bottles. A knock on the door sounded again and I sprinted to gather the Chinese food.

Kizzie left her jacket on the back of the couch. "You need help?" Kizzie asked.

"Yes, please. Can you get some plates?"

Separating everything on the table, I put my favorite orange chicken and stir fried rice on a plate.

Trisha poured sauce on her fried rice and egg rolls. "How much longer until your apartment is going to be ready?"

"Another week and then I'm back home."

"You don't seem too homesick."

I flipped my braids to the side and smiled.

"Girl look at that big ass hickey on her neck," Raven teased. I grabbed Shiva from running into her lap.

"The devil better keep her ass off my plate," Trisha fussed.

I rubbed the top of Shiva's head. "Leave my baby alone, Trisha. Your energy is throwing her off."

"Energy, my ass." Trisha guzzled the wine down and poured another glass.

"So both of you are dating friends! I'm so happy for you," Kizzie jested.

"Shut up, Kizzie," Trisha grumbled.

All of us burst into laughter and I slapped high-five with Kizzie. "At first I thought it would be bad for me and Caleb if we crossed that line."

"Normally as best friends it could turn bad, but you and Caleb know each other better than anyone. He's head over heels in love with you," Kizzie explained.

"I love him," I admitted.

"That means you have to work on the relationship and keep it fresh. Never let anything or anyone get in the middle. I'd hate to see you turn into Trisha and Lamar." Kizzie poked Trisha in the arm.

Trisha snatched up Shiva and sat back down. "Lamar is not my man."

"So what happened?"

Shiva started wiggling in her lap, wanting to play. Trisha tried to kiss her head, but Shiva pushed her paw to her lips. The girls and I chuckled at the frown on Trisha's face. "Why can't I kiss you, Shiva?" Trisha quizzed.

"Shiva knows your lips have run amuck," I laughed, the girls joining in on the jesting.

"She called him and another girl answered the phone," Raven revealed.

"Well, who she thought was another girl was actually his mom and she went off on her." Trisha put Shiva on the ground.

"You went off on his mom?"

Trisha glared at Raven. "I thought it was some bitch

playing on his phone, so I informed her that 'Bitch, you kissing my pussy when he kisses you'," Trisha said.

"What did his mom do?"

"She cursed me out," Trisha mumbled, throwing Shiva's toy on the ground for her to pick up.

"Lamar got you hooked."

"Same as Caleb got you glowing."

"He's my man and that's who I'm sticking with. We go together real bad." I stuck out my tongue and snapped my fingers excitedly. The girls laughed along with me and we continued catching up on each other's lives. Later in the evening, I drove to my parents' house, parking on the side of the street. I unbuckled my seatbelt and saw old man Roger sitting on the porch across the street with his pipe and cane.

"Hi, Mr. Roger. I thought the nurse said you couldn't smoke anymore?"

Roger took out his fake teeth. "Nobody runs me, baby. Get with me and I can change your life." He put them back in and the door opened wide to the nurse. He fumbled putting the cigar out and accidentally dropped it on his lap. He screamed in pain.

I giggled at him trying to flirt. "Mr. Roger, I am too young for you."

The nurse helped to clean up the mess. "What's going on with you, Kianna? You know I'm ready for you." Mr. Roger stood up, swinging his cane side to side and gyrating his hips. "Girl, keep on and you will miss out on this good stuff."

"Roger, sit your old butt down. My daughter is not interested!" Mom wrinkled her nose, yelling from the porch.

Mr. Roger stuck his tongue out. "Geraldine, shut up.

You might need some of this good loving to get your mind right."

"Calm down, Mr. Roger. You know my daddy goes crazy over my momma."

Roger stood in a fighting stance. "Tell your daddy I got time. He don't want none of this here." Roger started coughing, out of breath and taking out his asthma pump.

"Mr. Roger, you are hilarious." I walked into my parents' home, shutting the screen door behind my mom.

"Leave that old man alone." Mom put her hands on her hips.

I had come over to catch up with my family, but if she wanted to start nagging I would get up and leave. "Mr. Roger is a sweet old man. Hey, Daddy." I kissed him on the top of his head.

"What are you doing here?" Dad probed.

"Hanging out before Caleb comes home."

"I heard he has a new job out of state?" Dad asked.

I clasped my hands together in my lap. "We both got the job, but he's going to be out of state."

"Are you prepared to date someone long distance?" Mom interrupted, putting on her apron.

"We talked and we're going to make it work."

"I'm glad to hear that, pumpkin," Dad said, letting me lay my head on his shoulder.

"What smells good in the kitchen?"

"Your mom cooked all your favorites to celebrate you getting the job."

"Seriously? Geraldine Berry, the lady who constantly tells me I give her heartburn when I avoid church?"

Chuckling at my dramatics, Dad stood at the sound of the doorbell chiming. "The rest of the guests are here."

Dad hugged Mrs. Angel and shook hands with Mr. Glover.

"What are you two doing here?"

"Caleb called and told us the good news and we wanted to celebrate with you." Angel bent over to give me a hug and kiss.

"That's not necessary." I accepted the flowers and greeted his dad.

"Hush, child. When a man gives you flowers, you never decline," Angel schooled me and I agreed.

I giggled "Facts."

"Caleb is meeting us here," Mr. Glover relayed to us, and I remembered after lunch with the girls I didn't check my phone.

"Come on in the dining room. Food is almost ready." Mom gestured for everyone to take a seat around the table.

"Do you need help?" I questioned.

"Everything is ready. Just have to grab the biscuits," Mom replied.

Mrs. Glover took the seat across from me with Mr. Glover and left the empty chair for Caleb to sit right next to me.

"We are so proud of you, Kianna, on top of Caleb getting the job."

"Thank you."

"When do you start officially?" Mr. Glover guzzled his drink, then refilled his glass.

"In a week."

"Both our babies doing big things. Next will be the wedding," Mrs. Glover expressed with glee.

Choking on my water, I patted my chest. "It's way too early for a wedding."

"Girl, the way your hips are spreading we might have to speed up that wedding," Angel teased and caught eye contact with my mother as she fainted.

"Oh shit!" I jumped up, along with Mr. Glover, to check on my mom.

I gently checked her pulse and Mr. Glover grabbed the wet towel out of my dad's hand.

Caleb walked in at the wrong time. He helped my mom to stand. "What happened here Kianna?"

Mom grunted, rolling from side to side, mumbling how she went wrong with me at thirteen.

"Mom, don't worry. I am not pregnant."

"Pregnant!" Caleb shouted.

"Everybody calm down."

"Geraldine, where the hell are the keys to my car?" Mr. Roger burst through the house with the help of the nurse.

"Roger, now is not the time," Dad complained.

"What happened to her?" Roger pointed at my mom. The nurse and my mom worked together to keep him from trying to drive around when she's not here. So keeping his keys at our place was the best solution.

I sat Mom in the chair. My phone was ringing so I picked it up, only to hear the operator telling me the call was a collect call. "You have been reached by the Boston Trinity jail facilities, with a collect call from *Trisha*."

"What the hell Trisha!" I shouted after I accepted the call.

"Kianna, you have to help me," Trisha rushed out.

"My baby is pregnant and unmarried. Oh god!" Mom wailed and reached for her Bible.

"I've walked into a nightmare," Caleb moaned.

Chapter 9

Caleb

The dinner disaster ended with the ambulance coming to the Berrys' house. It was wrong, but I could not stop laughing at the chaos that followed Kianna. Once she got the phone call from Trisha, I drove her to help get her best friend bailed out, and then Trisha decided to go back to Lamar's house and make up with him. Kianna cursed both of them out and said to not get us involved in their mess anymore. I knew she would be right back listening to all the drama when she got bored. I was helping her move back into her place before my flight left for New York in two days. Our plan was to take things slow but go back and forth visiting as much as possible. After being in love with my best friend for so long, I would never allow anything to interrupt what we could build. She was on the same page as me for our future.

I put the paint brush back in the bucket and wiped the sweat off my forehead. Kianna decided to get all new furniture and repaint her bedroom to match the entire apartment since they changed the color scheme from the original. The damage from the flood had our landlord pissed, but when he heard about our newfound fame at the radio station, he wanted to flex a little and get free tickets to a lot of music and sports events in order to not put her out on the streets.

"Babe, can you help Lamar with the paintings?" Kianna asked.

"How much more stuff did you buy?"

"Two paintings and a few art pieces to set on the table," Kianna responded, moving her family photos around.

Shiva curled up around my leg. I picked her up and she plopped up on my shoulders, purring in my ear.

"Calm down, little momma."

"Shiva, that's my man." Kianna approached me, roping her arm around my waist.

"Shiva, you have to share me." I let her go and picked Kianna up. She automatically locked her arms around me.

"Come on, man. We don't want to hear that shit," Lamar grumbled, leaving more boxes on the floor. I pecked her lips and caressed her ass. I ignored him and walked us back to her bedroom.

"Y'all nasty!" Trisha barked, slamming the door. Kianna reached to take her shirt off and I laid her on the edge of the bed.

"She's right." I buried my head in her shoulder.

"I only have you for two more days." Kianna caressed the top of my head.

"Stop worrying, bug." I unbuckled my belt, dropped my pants on the ground, and pushed her to lie back on the bed.

"I already miss you," Kianna whispered. "Is that crazy?"

"I feel the same way." I slid my tongue over her clit. She trembled under my touch.

Her eyelids slammed shut. "Keep going, baby... please."

My baby's soft moans drove me wild and I prolonged her pleasure, nipping on her inner thigh, massaging her breasts.

"Fuck me now!"

"Give me what I want, Kianna!"

Smack!

The smack to her pussy sent a rush of lust into her eyes, and she bit down on her lip. "Come here." She motioned with her finger to come closer. She turned me onto my back, and I lined my dick up to her opening.

"You gonna miss me, baby," I warned her and kissed her hand.

I thrust upward, every muscle tensed with the need to own her, to possess her. My movements left her speechless. I grabbed a handful of her ass. I pulled her forward. Her breasts smothered me in the best way. I ran my tongue over each nipple. She threw her head back, a shiver covering her body.

"Keep bouncing. You take your dick, baby." The encouragement worked so well, she turned around reverse cowgirl, not releasing my stiff dick. I smacked her ass again, my fingers trailing up her back.

"Caleb! I love your dick so much."

"Fucking right."

Smack!

"Shit." I remained calm in front of her, but my breath stuttered and my eyebrows drew tight. I felt my orgasm as it was barreling down on me.

"Come with me, Caleb," Kianna begged.

I hurriedly circled my hips, stroked her two more times, then curled one hand around the back of her neck, and shoved my tongue in her mouth.

"Mmmmm. Miss you already," Kianna whined and fell back on the bed. I pulled her body flush to my chest and lifted her leg to slide back in for another round.

"Miss you more."

"Ahhh... fuck. We can't go all night, baby."

"Why the hell not?"

"My apartment is half done," her body shudder with a little giggle at me groping her breasts.

"Baby, ain't nobody interested in coming back after the way we left them. Furniture won't need to be moved since you'll only be moving from my dick."

That got a loud laugh out of her. We continued fucking for the rest of the afternoon and well into the night, only coming up for dinner. Only one day left to kick it together. All I wanted was to be over her, under her, and behind her.

* * *

"See, you already in love and shit." Lamar playfully pushed me on the side of my arm. I called the boys to play ball on the court for a few hours while Kianna went shopping with the girls.

"Try not to be a sour puss, since your girl ain't talking to you."

"Fuck Trisha and Jackie."

"How many you dealing with man?" Oscar passed the ball to me.

Lamar raised his hand and counted off. "At least four, but my favorites are Trisha and Jackie."

"Trisha gon beat your ass." I joked.

"Trisha might scare you two, but she knows I'm Daddy," Lamar claimed.

"From the phone call at the jail, you probably need to rethink your choices, bro."

"I mean Trisha is cool and all, but what you know about Raven?" Lamar asked.

"Hell nah! You ain't about to date friends, especially my girl's best friends," I lashed out, tossing the ball in the hoop.

"Ever since you and Kianna got together you soft, bro," Lamar muttered.

I slapped him on the back of the head. "Soft loving is what you need."

"My women know what time it is when I call," Lamar said with a smirk. Oscar and I made eye contact and laughed at his glare.

"Trisha had your ass crying when she avoided your calls. Stop fronting." Oscar said.

"Fuck you," Lamar responded.

"Leave that to Trisha." Oscar crossed him, passing the ball to our other friend, Glenn.

"You might need to give her some space."

Lamar stole the ball and dunked it in the hoop. "I'm a grown ass man. Trisha knew I don't do that one girl only shit."

Ignoring his rambling, I caught the ball, lining it up for a three- pointer. "Once I get settled, y'all can come visit."

"For sure. You moving to New York and all the single women." Lamar rubbed his hands together.

"I have a girl."

"Not talking about you, bro," Lamar said.

"Anyway, Kianna and I made plans to visit each other every other month, depending on schedules."

"Kianna's a good girl. You got it made, bro." Oscar went up for the ball.

"That's my baby."

"How much longer we gon talk about you and Kianna in love and shit?" Lamar blasted out, scowling at his cell phone.

"As long as I want. You all in your phone anyway. What'd Trisha do now?"

"The girls talking about going to the club and Trisha tagged me in the post," Lamar muttered.

"It's my last night in town. We should meet up."

"If I see her with some other dudes, I'm going off." Lamar grimaced, tucking the phone in his pocket.

"Leave that girl alone." I carried the ball to the benches and picked up my bottle of water.

"We doing the club?" Glenn inquired.

"Yeah, and leave your drama at home," I shouted at Lamar, watching him stalk off already yelling on his phone.

"That boy in love," Oscar joked, and I slapped hands with him, walking back to our cars. Two hours later we finally pulled up to the club, surprising the girls. And as usual Lamar and Trisha were doing the most. Kianna danced in my lap holding a glass to her lips. Oscar found him two girls to spend his time and money on. Glenn brought his longtime girlfriend, Cammie. Kianna said she wouldn't get too drunk for our last night together, so she could show off her tongue skills on my dick. That had me ready to go as soon as the words came out of her mouth. Even though it was a sad night for us, we still wanted to celebrate her starting at the radio in a new position. From what she told me, Cheston was impressed with the artist recommendations she had made.

"Babe, you hear me?"

"Sorry, what did you say?"

She poked her lip out in a pout. "I said let's go. All the girls got somebody, so we can sneak off."

"I thought you wanted to celebrate your promotion." I slid her braids behind her ear.

"I want some dick." Her brows hiked up, but she paused with a frown on her face.

"You are so spoiled, bug."

"I know." She chuckled, pressing a kiss to the side of my neck.

"Shit, girl. You got my dick hard again."

"Let's go home so I can take care you."

"You want to fly high with me, baby?"

"First class all the way."

Epilogue

Kianna

Sprinting through the airport, I made the turn to the escalator heading in the direction of his flight to meet him before he got off the plane. The past few months without him were hard and lonely, not being able to be in his presence, not only sleeping with him next to me, but waking up in his arms. I laughed at his jokes and listened to his words of encouragement and reveled in his praise for how well I was doing at my job. Caleb was more than just a best friend, more than a boyfriend. I would never be able to explain how he made me feel. I waved my hands as he came out of the line, rushing in my direction. He lifted me in the air, swung me around in a circle, and smashed his lips to mine.

"Mmmm. I take it you missed me."

He brushed a hand up and down my back. "I miss you every day, bug." Caleb put me down and linked our hands together.

"Is that your only carry-on bag?" I asked, seeing only the bookbag on his shoulder.

"That's what I wanted to talk to you about."

Stopping in my tracks, I hoped he wasn't giving me bad news at the start of our reunion. "Tell me."

"We can get in the car and talk."

"No, tell me now. Are you not staying for the weekend?"

"Of course, I am, but something else came up." Caleb grabbed one more bag from the luggage area, and he walked with me to the car.

"Tell me. Whatever you say, I promise not to kill you. Unless you cheated."

"Girl, shut up. Ain't nobody cheating." Caleb placed his bag in the back of his Jeep, that he'd left for me to use.

"I see you have another bag. What's really going on Caleb."

He started the car and grabbed my hand as he drove us out of the airport. I watched him clench the steering wheel.

"I talked with Cheston, and he offered me a new position."

"That's great honey! Wait, it is good, right?"

"The job is his position as the manager of the station."

"Hold up, are you saying you will be my new boss?"

He nodded. "Yeah, bug. I got great recommendations from my boss and when the position opened I applied, but I never thought he would offer it to me."

"So you're moving back home for good?"

"Yep, if you're cool with me as your boss."

"Umm...Hell yeah! Long lunch hours and sex before meetings."

He laughed at my jokes. "Bug, you're crazy."

"No, I am happy for you and glad you're home for good." I grazed my hand down the back of his neck.

"My mom already told your mom."

"Geraldine never told me."

Caleb arrived at our apartment building. "I made her promise to keep it to herself." He turned to me.

I felt a little naughty and looked around the parking area and saw it was empty. "So, she can keep a secret."

He nodded and licked his lips.

"Then we should celebrate." I crawled over to his lap and he pressed the button to put the seat back a little. I slowly slipped my hands under his shirt, kissing him on the side of his cheek, chin, and nose.

"Baby, you already know what you're asking for right now."

"I do."

"How did I get so lucky?"

"We earned each other. No luck was needed." I reached into his boxers and grasped his thick shaft. He groaned and I blushed at the way he felt underneath my palm.

"Something about you, Kianna Berry."

"Something about you, Caleb Glover."

I hope you enjoyed **Kianna** and **Caleb**, if you want to see more of these character check out bonus scenes here "https://chiquitadennie.squarespace.com/bonus-scenes , Ethan and Maya has a story to tell in **Bossy Billion-aire** here "https://bit.ly/3uB5oBC

Follow TN Seal Security series with a standalone, opposites attract, fake dating, military romance "**Nicco**" https://bit.ly/47ZZN6p Are you a fan of sports romance? Then download one-night stand, billionaire romance "**Refuel**"https://bit.ly/3RqFx8l Also, follow it up with workplace, sports romance "**Pressure**" https://bit.ly/3RqagT1_If you love romantic comedy, fake relationships, enemies to lovers, find it here, "**Something Gained.**" Click the link https://bit.ly/3OwGbiP. My stories of friends finding love started with the Heart of Stone series that includes a host of characters and family. "**Broken**" book 1 Emery and Jackson a sports, one night stand, workplace romance is here:https://bit.ly/3hxVavF

Then you can continue with a fun side story of Emery and Jackson with "**Valentine's Day short** here:https://bit.ly/42ttg7o

Jordan, her best friend's story, continues here in "**Rebirth**" book 2 a single dad, widow billionaire romance here:https://bit.ly/3YiQtGS Hope on and download "**Reveal**" with Angela and Brent https://bit.ly/3OupYur If you love bonus content click here "https://chiquitadennie.squarespace.com/bonus-scenes

* * *

Please also check out a second-chance workplace romance here, "**Renew Book 4**"https://bit.ly/3worgHi with a host of characters intertwined.

Follow Desiree and Gabriel in "**Temptation**" a standalone contemporary, sports, curvy girl romance. Check it out herehttps://bit.ly/42r8ODQ

Check out dark mafia romance here that started my journey with Antonio and Sabrina in "**Ruthless Book 1**"https://bit.ly/3iS64XT

The relationship continues in "**Savage**" book 2 as

they get to know each other and their families:https://bit.ly/3w77CJT

Antonio and Sabrina have more work to do in "**Beast**" book 3 right here:https://bit.ly/3Untivm

* * *

Did you know **Janice** and **Carlo** have a book? Well grab this dark mafia romance with emotional scars, and betrayal right here:https://bit.ly/42yJBaH

Any fans of forbidden romance, political? Check out "**Mutual Agreement**"https://bit.ly/3OyAzod a steamy romance. Do you love workplace romantic suspense? Then check out "**Aydin**" https://bit.ly/496jKcv and the interconnected standalone hate to love, actress, damsel in distress bodyguard romance "**Nasir**" click the link here https://bit.ly/3uovwQr

Have you checked out "**She's All I Need**" click here https://books2read.com/u/49lkeW a sports, opposites attract romance. What about dark romance that has everything from steamy romance, opposites attract, suspense, thriller, celebrity, and more "**Stolen Book 1**" https://books2read.com/u/mvZlgV Don't miss the follow up Joaquin and Sofia's story in book 2 "**Saved**" https://books2read.com/u/4DWwLd

The conclusion for Joaquin and Sofia comes full circle in "**Betrayed**" here: https://books2read.com/u/4A5LGp

* * *

Catch up with favorite characters in this holiday short

romance which includes spoilers. "**Holiday collection**" here https://books2read.com/u/bzd59G

For small town, single mom stories check out "**Until Seren**a" https://books2read.com/u/mej8vr. Always fun when you love billionaire romances so check in with "**Cocky Catcher**" a sports romance, enemies to lovers here https://bit.ly/3R57VeT

A reader of sports workplace romance? Grab "**Scoring with Sadie**" a workplace, enemies to lovers romance here:https://bit.ly/3nkWhBp All curvy girl, plus size romance lovers get into "**I Deserve His Love**" a standalone, second chance romance here: https://books2read.com/u/mVrGwP

The fantasy romance readers look no further than a "**Red Light District**" a curvy girl, fling romance here: https://books2read.com/u/m2RQ6G

About the Author

Chiquita Dennie is an author of Contemporary, Romantic Suspense, Erotic, and Women's Fiction.

Chiquita lives in Los Angeles, CA. Before she started writing contemporary romance, she worked in the entertainment industry on notable TV shows such as the Dr. Phil show, the Tyra Banks show, American Idol, and Deal or No Deal. But her favorite job is the one she's now doing: full-time writing romance.

A best-selling author and award-winning filmmaker, her first short film, "Invisible," was released in summer 2017 and screened in multiple festivals and won for Best Short Film. She also hosts a podcast that showcases the latest in beauty, business, and community called "Moscato and Tea." Her debut release of *Antonio and Sabrina Struck in Love* has opened a new avenue of writing that she loves. Nominated for 2021 Author of the Year, Best Black Romance "Mutual Agreement," and Best Interracial Romance for "She's All In Need". In 2022 nominated Author Queen of the Year, Best Black Romance "Nasir" Best Interracial Romance "Torn" and Best Romantic Comedy "Something Gained" by Black Girls Who Write.

If you want to know when the next book will come out, please visit my website at http://www.chiquitadennie.com, where you can sign up to receive an email for my next release.

Struck of Love Universe

The Early Years-A Prequel
https://books2read.com/u/49Zjnw
Ruthless Struck In Love Book 1
https://books2read.com/u/4AxKL0
Savage Struck In Love Book 2
https://books2read.com/u/bpED6g
Beast Struck In Love Book 3
https://books2read.com/u/3LpgdJ
Janice and Carlo Captivated By His Love
https://books2read.com/u/b6je6M
Brutal Struck In Love Book 4
https://books2read.com/u/4NQyE9
Stolen-Fuertes Mafia Cartel Book 1
https://books2read.com/u/mvZlgV
Saved-Fuertes Mafia Cartel Book 2
https://books2read.com/u/4DWwLd
Redemption Struck In Love Book 5
https://books2read.com/u/b5kZ8O
Betrayal- Fuertes Mafia Cartel Book 3
https://books2read.com/u/4A5LGp

Torn: The Carrington Cartel Book 1
https://books2read.com/u/mqXare?utm_source=
universal+link
Claim: The Carrington Cartel Book 2
https://books2read.com/u/bwyjPY

Heart of Stone Universe

Broken 1 Emery and Jackson
https://books2read.com/u/boWPAV
Heart of Stone Book 1.5
https://payhip.com/b/kWg7
Rebirth 2 Jordan and Damon
https://books2read.com/u/ba2OMx
Heart of Stone Book 3.5 Bottoms Up
https://payhip.com/b/HGP1
Reveal 3 Angela and Brent
https://books2read.com/u/31rx9l
Renew 4 Jessica and Joseph
https://books2read.com/u/4NXyPG

Also By Chiquita Dennie

Series

Struck in Love
The Early Years-A Prequel Short Story
Ruthless:Antonio and Sabrina Book 1
Savage: Antonio and Sabrina Book 2
Beastl: Antonio and Sabrina Book 3
Captivated By His Love:Janice and Carlo
Brutal: Antonio and Sabrina Booke 4
Redemption: Antonio and Sabrina Book 5

Heart of Stone
Broken, Book 1 (Emery & Jackson)
A Valentine's Day Short Book 1.5 Emery & Jackson
Rebirth, Book 2 (Jordan and Damon)
Reveal, Book 3 (Angela and Brent)
Bottoms Up Book 3.5 Jessica and Joseph Short
Renew, Book 4 (Jessica and Joseph)

Cocky Billionaire Boys

Cocky Catcher (Cocky Billionaire Boys Book 1)
Bossy Billionaire (Cocky Billionaire Boys Book 2)

The Fuertes Cartel

Stolen (The Fuertes Cartel Book 1)
Saved (The Fuertes Cartel Book 2)
Betrayed (The Fuertes Cartel Book 3)

Carrington Cartel

Torn: The Carrington Cartel Book 1
Claim: The Carrington Cartel Book 2

Something

Something Gained: A Romantic Comedy Book 1
Something Earned: A Romantic Comedy Book 2

Pierce Motors

Refuel:(Pierce Motors Book l)
Pressure:(Pierce Motors Book 2)

Summer Break

Summer Nights(Summer Break Book 1)

TN Seal Security

Aydin: Book 1
Nasir: Book 2
Nicco: Book 3

Standalones

Until Serena(HEA World Novel)
Temptation
She's All I Need

I Deserve His Love
Mutual Agreement
Scoring with Sadie
Exposed (A Bodyguard Novel)
Love Shorts:A Collection of Short Stories
Red Light District(A Fantasy Romance Short)

<u>By Keke Renée:</u>
Wet Heat
His Peace, Her Pleasure
Baby, It's Cold Outside
Love Don't Live Here Anymore, Book 1, 2
Every Time We Touch (A Wet Heat Novelette)
One Night Only- Love By Design Book 1
Cassian and Savannah Love By Design Book 2
Deidra's Love -Love By Design Book 3
Protecting Bria: Book 1
Protecting Chanel:Book 2
Protecting Yanira: Book 3
Haven: A Single Dad Romance
Sensual
Seek to Please: Book 1
Seek To Touch: Book 2
Seek To Bare:Book 3
Seek To Love: Book 4
Seek To Trust: Book 5
Seek To Earn: Book 6
Tease Me: Book 1
Promise Me: Book 1

<u>By Ava S.King</u>
Fatal Memory: Book 1 Teagan Stone
Fatal Target: Book 2 Teagan Stone

Fatal Crime: Book 3 Teagan Stone
Fatal Justice: Book 4 Teagan Stone
Fatal Enemy: Book 5 Teagan Stone
Fatal Death: Book 6 Teagan Stone
Fatal Revenge: Book 7 Teagan Stone
Fatal Pursuit: Book 8 Teagan Stone
Mirror of Lies: Book 1
Mirror of Lust: Book 2
Ruined: Andi Easton Book 1

Thank you so much for reading and if you enjoyed the crazy ride and decide to leave a review we'd truly appreciate the support..

What's Next?

Want to know what happens next?

Follow me on social media to catch the next release.

Reviews are the lifeblood of the publishing world. They're read, appreciated, and needed. Please consider taking the time to leave a few words on Goodreads, or bookbub.

Sign up for updates and sneak peaks at the site below.
https://www.bookbub.com/chiquitadennie
https://www.chiquitadennie.com
https://www.goodreads.com/author/chiquitadennie
https://Facebook.com/chiquitassteamyreadinggroup
x.com/authorchiquitad
https://www.instagram.com/authorchiquitadennie
https://www.Facebook.com/authorchiquitadennie
https://www.304publishing.tumblr.com

304 Publishing Company

We showcase authors writing Romance, Women's Fiction, Thriller, and Erotic.Along with Mystery, Suspense, Poetry, Beauty, and Style Books. Thank you for taking the time out to visit. Join our mailing list to stay updated with new releases and blog posts.

Acknowledgments

A huge thank you to my team that helps me behind the scenes, from my editors, test readers, graphic designers, and the list goes on. Truly appreciate each of you for keeping me on my toes.

www.ingramcontent.com/pod-product-compliance
Lightning Source LLC
Chambersburg PA
CBHW071945190726
48293CB00004B/1355